Navajo Autumn

R. Allen Chappell

DEDICATION

Writing a book is a solitary game yet often requires a certain amount of cheering from the sidelines. This book is dedicated to those who kept the faith and, in the process, convinced me to do likewise. I suspect there are many manuscripts hidden away in desk drawers whose writers have not been so fortunate.

Table of Contents

Preface

Though this book is a work of fiction, a concerted effort was made to maintain the accuracy of the culture and characters. There are many scholarly tombs written by anthropologists, ethnologists, and learned laymen regarding the Navajo culture. On the subject of language and spelling, they often do not agree. When no consensus was apparent we have relied upon "local knowledge."

Many changes have come to the *Dinè*—some of them good; some, not so much. These are the Navajos I remember. I think you may like them.

~~~~~~

This story hearkens back to a slightly more traditional time on the reservation, and while the places and culture are real, the characters and their names are fictitious. Any resemblance to actual persons living or dead is purely coincidental.

ACKNOWLEDGMENTS

Many sincere thanks to those Navajo friends and class-mates who provided "grist for the mill." Their insight into Navajo thought and reservation life helped fuel a lifelong interest in their culture that I had once only observed from the other side of the fence.

1

SPIDER WOMAN

Just outside Farmington, New Mexico, the San Juan River swings in close to the highway to pick up a tributary at the mouth of a wide, nearly dry, streambed—La Plata, it's called—not much more than a trickle usually, though it can be more if they get any rain up-country. The day they found Patsy Greyhorse's body, it was just a trickle.

Nothing extraordinary in that. Navajos dead beside the highway are not uncommon in that country—drunk, some of them, wandering around in traffic at night, their eyes not reflecting the headlights like a deer or a horse.

Three things took this particular instance out of the ordinary: Patsy Greyhorse was not a Navajo, she had not been drinking, and she was very highly placed in the Bureau of Indian Affairs.

Thomas Begay, on the other hand—who was found sleeping under the bridge nearby—was a Navajo (drunk unfortunately) and of very unsavory character. It was only natural that the sheriff's deputy should immediately arrest him, and by order of his superiors, cause Thomas to be taken to the county hospital for blood tests and evaluation. He arrived even before the remains of Patsy Greyhorse.

Thomas Begay, at twenty-nine years old, had never been inside a hospital even when being born. That un-noteworthy event took place in a summer hogan north of Tuba City. While his present surroundings were strange, the smell of the hospital was familiar, putting him in mind of the B.I.A dormitories and classrooms that were a sinister part of his childhood. Government school—he wouldn't wish it on a dog. He had suffered no more than his father before him of course, but that had not made it any easier for Thomas Begay.

He couldn't see any good coming from this county hospital, even though he had a fearsome headache, vision blurring in rhythm with each labored breath—trouble getting enough air, as though a steel band was drawn tight about his chest. Surely, he thought, a man of twenty-nine couldn't be having a heart attack. There had been innumerable hangovers, but nothing like this. He was sober enough now to know he had been arrested but was still uncertain as to why. No matter, he had been arrested on a number of occasions, and, while never pleasant, he had come to accept it as the way in which he paid for the life he led—which is to say a very bad life indeed if you were to listen to talk on the reservation.

Thomas Begay lived with his ex-mother-in-law, a thing hard to understand if you are white. Should you be Navajo, however, it would be so horrific, so unfathomable as to generate outrage and disgust of monumental proportions. In the old times a man was not allowed even to look upon his mother-in-law, let alone speak to her. And here was Thomas Begay living with Lucy Tallwoman, whose daughter had left after one pitiful year of marriage. The girl, in shame, had left that part of the reservation and was said to be working in a back-alley bar in Gallup. She refused to discuss her mother or ex-husband, even when drinking, which she often was.

It should be mentioned that Lucy Tallwoman was an unusually good-looking woman for her age, which was probably no more than thirty-eight. A cheerful, hardworking weaver of blankets in the traditional manner—blankets bringing extremely high collector prices—making Lucy Tallwoman quite well off, relatively speaking. She did not drink.

She had borne her daughter out of wedlock when she was eighteen, the result of an unfortunate infatuation with a white music teacher at boarding school. That her daughter was part white was undeniable. It had been an unlucky mix in most people's view as the daughter was quite plain and given to fits of depression. Thomas Begay, a fine-looking young man and one of great wit and charm when sober, attributed his young wife's moodiness to this white blood and was prone to make excuses for her on that basis. (All this according to the local trader who was well up on the situation, having had an eye for Lucy Tallwoman and her blankets himself.)

~~~~~~

Thomas Begay sat handcuffed to the chromium arm of an emergency room lounge chair, mesmerized by a small brown spider that was lowering itself from the ceiling to the potted plant beside him. The deputy had hurried away to look for the E.R. nurse as there was no one at the check-in desk when they arrived.

"Hurry up, hurry up," Thomas thought vaguely as he watched the spider, "That's the white way." It was not a common spider, and Thomas Begay was trying to focus on it. Something about the way it hovered there at eye level, twirling this way and that on its silver strand, made him think of Spider Woman and the strange things his grandfather had told him as a child.

"Is that you, Spider Woman?" Thomas whispered, peering blearily at the little creature. "Have you come for me?" He leaned over the arm of the chair to better hear what the Spider Woman might have to say. As he put his full weight on the chair arm, he couldn't help but notice that the weld holding it to the frame was not really welded at all, but had broken loose at some time in the past and was now held together only by the tension of the frame's curvature.

Thomas Begay studied this new development, carefully adjusting his weight back and forth, watching the weld separate at the nearly indiscernible hairline crack. It finally dawned on him that indeed Spider Woman had come for him and that he had best be cooperating. Putting all his weight against the arm, he slipped off the steel ring and sat looking at his cuffed hand, now in his lap. "Thank you, Spider Woman," he said quietly, rising unsteadily to his feet. His head felt much better while he was standing, and his breath came more easily too. Looking both ways down the hall, he put the manacled hand in his jacket pocket and moved away, opposite the direction taken by the deputy.

Coming out the back entrance of the hospital into the morning light, Thomas Begay's eyes fell upon the patrol car. Surely the keys wouldn't—but they were, and as he pulled out of the parking lot, he shook a finger in the rearview mirror and said, "You see how it is when you hurry up, hurry up all the time!"

The hospital stands at the edge of town on a hill above the river, and across the river, over the bridge, lie more than twenty-five thousand square miles of the Navajo reservation—possibly the largest Indian reservation in the world. The tribal council now refers to it as the "Navajo

Nation." Older Indians still refer to it as *Dine' Bikeyah* "Navajo Country" but young people just call it "the Res." Even today a person can become lost in its vastness, disappear, so to speak, should they be of a mind.

Thomas Begay drove very slowly in that overly cautious manner drunk people assume when trying to appear sober. As he crossed the bridge, he noticed the water was low, exposing large piles of driftwood which had collected against the buttresses, including a few cottonwood trees of considerable size.

~~~~~~

Navajos as a rule are not good swimmers, and Thomas hated the very thought of it. The cold water caused him to suck in his breath, though it was quite shallow—four feet at the most. Easing along underneath the bridge until he reached the driftwood, he selected the broken-off top of a cottonwood tree that still had some upper branches and even leaves attached. Pushing it out into the river, he floated alongside, his body submerged, his head hidden in the leaves, the toes of his tennis shoes bouncing softly along the rocky bottom. Far away in the distance, he could hear the faint wail of sirens. He smiled to himself through chattering teeth. *They will search every arroyo from the river to the bluffs before they think of the water.* And of course he was right.

~~~~~~

Charlie Yazzie was investigating the disappearance of four sheep and an Angora goat over in Hunter's Wash when the call came from headquarters, touching off the horn alarm on his vehicle. He would not ordinarily have been called out for missing sheep except that the complaint had come from his grandmother Mary Plenty Goats, who had specifically requested her grandson. Sue Hanagarni, who was on the switchboard at the time, had gone to high school with Charlie and thought it would be a fine joke to put the report through on the air. "...Yes, Charlie, your grandmother says Samuel Shorthair already came out but that he can't find his ass with both hands. She wants those animals back. The goat is due to kid-out any time, and it's that good one you bought her at the fair last fall." Sue Hanagarni was laughing so hard now she had to turn off the microphone but not before Charlie heard Pete Fish in the background, "This is the big one Charlie! Show them what you can do." Charlie would hear about this for a while.

Charlie often talked about the "Big One"—the case that would someday come along and make legal services sit up and take notice, the one that would be his ticket into the law offices where he rightly belonged. Graduating law school at the University Of New Mexico the previous fall, Charlie had found the only thing available on the reservation was this special investigator position—just another fancy name for a legal department gofer as far as Charlie was concerned. "Legal staffs full up," said the interviewer, a heavy-set Bitter Water clan woman with thick glasses. "We'll give you a call as soon as something turns up. Just hang in there."

It had been nearly a year now and Charlie was still hanging. What made the situation even more depressing was that he had virtually no options. Interviewing with several private firms in Farmington had shown there was little chance of an Indian being hired outside the reservation. White clients would be leery of an Indian attorney, and the Indians, of course, would avail themselves of the legal services offered by the tribe. This was the dilemma facing many graduating Navajo professionals. That was just the way it was. But Charlie didn't have to like it.

Sue Hanagarni had been much more serious the second time she called. She had given him everything they had on

Patsy Greyhorse and told him about Thomas Begay escaping in the deputy sheriff's patrol unit. Charlie could tell she was excited. "There's an inter-agency meeting in Farmington in one hour, and you're the only one close enough to get there in time. The boss says go for it! ...And Charlie," she added with a touch of awe in her voice, "this really might be the big one."

"Inter-agency meeting" meant the Feds would be there, along with the state patrol, the sheriff's office of course, and probably the local police too. Charlie wondered if the sheriff would have the nerve to show up himself or send a deputy, maybe even the one that let Thomas Begay escape.

Thomas Begay—again? It had been only last week that he had given him a friendly warning about driving without a license. It had been on a back road on the reservation between Lucy Tallwoman's camp and the trading post. Charlie hadn't wanted to make a big deal of it. Technically, Thomas really hadn't been driving at all, just passed out in the truck which was nosed over in the ditch beside the road.

He had known Thomas a long time, had, in fact, always liked him. Like Sue Hanagarni and himself, Thomas had gone to school at the same government boarding facilities. He had been one of the brightest boys in their class and an all-state quarterback. It just seemed that nothing ever turned out right for Thomas. He had knocked around the reservation for the last few years working as a mechanic, then construction on several government projects. After marrying a girl no one knew from over around Shiprock, he took to doing some serious drinking. A year later he was separated and living with his mother-in-law.

"Whew!" Charlie thought, rubbing his forehead. "You just never know." Thomas Begay didn't seem the type. He glanced at his watch, reaching down to hit the flashers, kicking it up to seventy, which he thought he could get away with, at least on the reservation.

Charlie was late despite it all and ran up the steps of the federal building and into the conference room in time to hear sheriff's deputy Dudd Schott telling the assemblage how Thomas Begay had wrenched the arm off a lounge chair in order to make his escape, using car keys he had obviously lifted from Dudd's belt on the way into the hospital. Dudd's face was livid, and his little pig-eyes darted from person to person during the telling as if daring anyone to question any part of it. One of the FBI agents, a small but distinguished-looking man in a three-piece, pinstripe, held up a hand and asked if the keys to the handcuffs had been on the car ring. Dudd beamed triumphantly and said, "You bet your ass they weren't," digging in his uniform pocket and producing the keys in question. "That navvy will be wearing those bracelets for a while, I expect."

The federal agent, nodding thoughtfully, stood up, and, noticing Charlie, motioned him to a chair at the end of the table. "So, Gentlemen, let me reiterate briefly what we have here so far...and I must say it isn't much." The agent went over the sheriff's report, calling to their attention that Patsy Greyhorse was a Sioux woman recently appointed by the BIA to look into certain dealings within the Navajo tribe. She was an expert on water rights and acquisition and was to have delivered a report to a tribal conference the previous night in Window Rock. She had last been seen at her motel where she was to freshen up before meeting acquaintances for lunch. Her body had been spotted by a passing tourist from Ohio, who had stopped at 6:15 that morning to relieve himself beside the La Plata Bridge. How she had wound up over a hundred miles to the north was just one of the unanswered questions. There would be an information package for each of them at the end of the conference, including a preliminary coroner's report, pictures (including file photos of Thomas Begay), and more background on Patsy Greyhorse. The agent asked if there were any further questions, looking slightly irritated when Charlie Yazzie held up his hand. "Yes?"

"Excuse me ...I arrived late. Could you tell me how close Thomas Begay was to the body when apprehended?" The federal agent pointed a finger at Dudd Schott, who frowned as he looked over at Charlie whom he knew slightly and considered much too uppity for an Indian.

"He was passed out under the bridge when I found him maybe ten-fifteen feet from the body, but he had blood on his shirt and his face was scratched. The deputy hesitated, "It's all in the report." The thought of an Indian being a special investigator with a law degree annoyed Dudd, who had barely made it through the New Mexico Police Academy, even with the help of his wife's cousin, who was on the examining board. He and Charlie had bumped heads several times in the past when Dudd had been harassing Indians around town. The Indians referred to him as "Deputy Dog" and laughed behind his back. Dudd knew Charlie had no jurisdiction outside the reservation, just as Dudd had very little inside. The federal agent in charge dismissed the meeting with a final notation that Washington was "quite concerned and expected no stone to be left unturned."

Dudd Schott caught up with Charlie in the parking lot. "Where you reckon that little bastard Begay will head for?" He was wheezing from the short run across the lawn. Dudd didn't care for Indians in general, and it irritated him to have to call on one for help. That back-to-the-blanket sonofabitch Thomas Begay would pay for making him out to be a fool.

Charlie stopped and looked Dudd square in his fat face, causing Dudd to turn even redder. "The reservation," he said quietly, turning his back on him.

As Charlie drove off, Dudd was still standing in the parking lot, red-faced and glaring. "No-talkin' sons-a-bitches," he wheezed.

Charlie really didn't know exactly where Thomas Begay might go for sure, but it would be somewhere on the reservation all right—that's where all Navajos head when they are in trouble. He didn't mind Dudd knowing. Dudd had little jurisdiction there. Only federal and tribal officers held any real authority on the reservation.

~~~~~~

Lucy Tallwoman patted her old father's knee as they drove away from the supermarket. "Well, we got everything you like," she said hopefully in Navajo. "Strawberry cream soda, canned tomatoes, and Oreo cookies," enumerating these last items in English as that was easier. The old man gave no sign that he heard or approved of the purchases. He was nearly seventy-five years old and of that contrary frame of mind old people sometimes fall into. She had been late this morning picking him up for their regular Sunday outing, and he was not in the mood to overlook it.

"Look there!" she gestured. "Someone has brought a horse and wagon to town. You certainly don't see that much anymore." The old man lifted his head in momentary interest. He looked at the old couple driving the spring-wagon in mild surprise.

"I know those people," he said, slowly turning in his seat. "Those are the people who used to live down by Nageezi trading post in the sand wash. I went to help out at a Sing there a long time ago, a Night Chant for their son who was very sick...even helped with the sand painting ...that was when I was still studying to be *Hataalii.*" He shook his head sadly, looking down at his hands. "The Night Chant is a long sing...on the last day the boy died."

Lucy looked over at her father, pursing her lips thoughtfully. "Well, they must live around here now. They didn't drive that wagon very far I bet. Do you wanna stop and say hello? We got plenty of time."

The old man looked at his daughter as though she might be dull witted. "No! Don't stop...I told you...their son died."

Lucy shrugged her shoulders and turned the battered pickup truck onto the highway, south toward the great Shiprock.

She hoped Thomas Begay would be waiting at the La Plata Bridge. He hadn't been there this morning, though that was where she usually picked him up after one of his all-nighters. She hadn't stopped to look under the bridge coming into town this morning. If he was under there, it would mean he was still drunk, and she didn't care to deal with that. When he sobered up, he would be standing by the bridge waiting for a ride, if not from her, from someone who didn't know him. That might take a while.

"Where is Thomas?" the old man suddenly asked as though reading her mind. "Is he drunk?" The old man took a perverse pleasure in needling her about Thomas Begay and his drinking. He did this, she supposed, in retaliation for the shame she had brought upon the family. The truck squealed as she pushed in the clutch, looking for the last gear. Something about the throw-out bearing, Thomas had said. That's what's making it squeal. This truck wouldn't last much longer. One of these days it would just lay down on them like an old horse, and that would be the end of it. She had enough money put away for a better truck when the time came, but she wanted to get all the good out of this one first. Lucy Tallwoman was not frivolous with her money—Thomas Begay being the only luxury she afforded herself.

~~~~~~

Thomas Begay was becoming painfully sober as he floated inexorably down the river, hidden among the branches of the cottonwood. Never had he suffered such a hangover. He felt like he had been run over, chemically speaking. The cold green water of the San Juan lapped at his trembling lips, and he sipped a little from time to time to ease his parched throat and pounding head.

His hands, pale and wrinkled, clutched at the tree branches in front of his face. His legs, numb from the waist down, could no longer feel his feet bumping along the bottom. It was only a few miles from the hospital bridge to the confluence of the San Juan and La Plata, and he forced himself to watch the western shoreline for signs of the approaching juncture. If he could maintain his frigid grip on the log, he would, at some point, swing in very close to where his drunken slumber had been so rudely interrupted earlier in the morning.

He studied the face of his black plastic watch through the swirling water. The American flag on the dial seemed to be waving in the current, and the little second hand was clicking along splendidly. "These watches really could take a licking and keep on ticking," he thought. The watch, a blue light special, had been a good buy at $14.95, and yet Lucy Tallwoman had chided him for his extravagance. It crossed his mind that maybe sometime he would write the company a little note telling them of his experience with their product and maybe be on one of those TV commercials—maybe they could have a stuntman do this part in the river. It appeared to be only ten o'clock according to the squiggly black hands, which meant only three hours had passed since his arrest, and here he had come nearly full circle. Soon Lucy Tallwoman would be coming by on her way home with the groceries and her father. They would be looking to pick him up as they had done in the past. He had no more than thought this when the river began its slight bend to the West, and in the distance he could see, suspended between cobalt sky and a shimmer of golden cottonwoods, the shining concrete of the La Plata Bridge.

~~~~~~

Lucy Tallwoman pulled the old truck across the traffic lane to the riverside of the road and parked on the pull-off just before the bridge. She sat there a moment in the warm October sun, listening to the rhythmic ticking of the engine as it cooled. Her father, who had been dozing, opened one eye; looking around, he immediately recognized the bridge as their pick-up point for Thomas Begay. "So, where is Bad-boy Begay?" he said in English, using his made-up name for Thomas. "Still passed out under the bridge?"

"I don't know. I haven't looked under the bridge yet," Lucy Tallwoman replied, leaning her head out the window, tapping the fingers of her left hand on the roof of the truck. She was beginning to hope that Thomas Begay had already hitched a ride with someone foolish enough to stop, though she considered this unlikely. "Look! There's a police car up ahead and some men measuring or surveying or something down in the wash." She shot the old man a concerned look. "You don't think something has happened to Thomas, do you?"

"I doubt they would be measuring Thomas," the old man replied, "...much as I would like to hear it." He stared straight ahead, "Do you want me to go look under the bridge?" He spoke more gently now and turned to his daughter with a half-smile. "Maybe a little kick from behind will get him started off right this morning."

Lucy Tallwoman smiled back. "I'm sure you would enjoy that, but for the sake of peace on a Sunday morning, I'll go look for Thomas Begay." As she reached for the door handle, there came a hiss from the underbrush, causing her to jump, hitting her head on the window frame. "Psst!" It came again—a sound so pronounced that even her father's old ears had no trouble hearing it.

The old man rolled his eyes heavenward, shaking his head. "Tell me it's a snake and not Thomas," he sighed.

Lucy Tallwoman peered into the brush beside the truck. Some branches rattled, and twigs with leaves began to move upward out of the bar-ditch. "Don't move," the twigs whispered. "Don't say anything. Act regular."

Lucy turned to her father. "It's him," she said in a small voice. "He has twigs on his head."

"Now what?" the old man said in a tired whisper. "Has he gone completely away, or what?"

"Get out and pretend to check the oil," the twigs said, almost at the edge of the road. "Leave your door open and the hood up until I'm inside."

Lucy Tallwoman, sensing the urgency in Thomas Begay's voice, moved to the front of the truck, leaving her door open and blocking the view from up the road. She was beginning to piece things together. Covertly, she looked toward the police car as she raised the hood and played at checking the oil. She watched, fascinated, as the pile of brush slithered up from the ditch and into the floorboards of the truck. Trying not to hurry, doing her best to appear nonchalant, she closed the hood and climbed back into the driver's side of the truck She did not look at the mass of twigs and leaves, even now, sticking up above the dash-board. Her father sat quietly, peering at her through the thin screen of foliage that now separated them. She shook her head at him, placing a forefinger to her lips. The pile of twigs shuddered with relief as the truck pulled out onto the highway and crossed the bridge for home. No one looked at the men with the measuring devices.

2

`THE GUN`

Charlie Yazzie's government truck was playing one of its old familiar tricks—the engine cutting in and out, sputtering, choking, forcing Charlie to shift down into second gear and rev the motor unmercifully. He hated it when it did this. It put him on edge to know that he might have to walk out of the backcountry; it was inevitable of course, just a matter of time, as they say. The truck was an agency hand-me-down, far past its prime. The reservation roads had already taken their toll. The people in charge of the motor pool had done their best but couldn't seem to pinpoint the problem, couldn't seem to tell if it was in the electrical or the fuel system, though Charlie had insisted it was the former. It would never act up on test drives, only when Charlie was forty miles from nowhere. And forty miles from nowhere was where he was now.

He had chosen to take the back way into Lucy Tallwoman's camp, hoping to avoid detection on the long open flats leading to their camp from the highway. This road, trail really, ran up Big Sand Wash and came in from the high hills behind the camp, allowing him to remain hidden, maybe slip up on them. Oh, they would be on the lookout all right, but hell, he was an Indian too. Charlie's clan was *Bit'ahnii*, the Within-His-Cover-People. If he couldn't slip up on them, who could?

He was still two, maybe three miles from the camp when the truck finally gave up, lurching to a choking halt in a slight depression in the wash.

Charlie cursed in English as there are no really good Navajo curse words. "You sorry sonofabitch," he said, getting out of the truck. "No good bastard!" Charlie had always preferred Chevrolets, and his resolve was now strengthened in that direction. He kicked the truck in the driver's side door and scooping up a rock, flung it through the open window. Some people thought Charlie Yazzie a little high-strung for a Navajo. "I'm going to get me a new Chevy," he whispered, gritting his teeth, knowing it to be an idle threat. After walking around the vehicle several times, saying bad things to it in Navajo, Charlie calmed down enough to get in and try the two-way radio. Nothing. The radio was dead. "So, it is in the electrical!" Charlie allowed himself a grim smile of satisfaction at this.

He sat there, his mind a clutter, thinking what to do, thinking about Lucy Tallwoman and Thomas Begay. *Why did these people still isolate themselves so, clinging to the old things, the old manner of living?* Charlie had spent so long a time away at school that he had forgotten much of the old ways, leaving a vague dissatisfaction with those who would not better themselves. He thought of Patsy Greyhorse. Now there was a modern Indian—head of a government committee in Washington, traveling all over the country, looking into important issues. There was a life a person could take pride in, a way to be somebody, to make a difference. Why did these people want to live out here with no running water, no electricity, herding sheep for a living—if it could be called a living. They had been to school, seen the things the *Billigaana* way had to offer. Still they clung to this hard life and their superstitious ways. There was no accounting for it, he thought.

Sliding over to the passenger side, he opened the glove box and pulled out a revolver, a .38 S&W Chief's Special with turquoise set grips. It had been a present from his family when he became an investigator. It was stainless steel. "You can store this thing in a toilet tank if you want to," the salesman told them. "It's totally impervious to rust." None of them had a toilet tank, but they smiled and agreed that might come in handy sometime. They had visions of Charlie rounding up a lot of crooks with that gun. Wrong.

He had fired it only a few times at some tin cans. He was not a very good shot. Rummaging further in the glove box, he came up with just four cartridges which he inserted into the cylinder, easing the hammer down on the one empty chamber. The 125-grain slugs gave a nice little heft to the gun, and he spun it on his trigger-finger to get the feel of it. Charlie had no intention of shooting anyone. It just seemed to be the professional thing to do, having this gun. Four bullets would be plenty, he thought.

Sneaking through the cedars and scrub oak, he worked his way through the dry, grey hills and gullies in the gathering dusk. He was going on dead reckoning now, trusting his intuition. He was sure the Tribal Police had already been there, but he was just as sure that they had not found Thomas Begay. Thomas was too smart for that. He would stay away from the camp during the day and would be watching the road coming in from the highway at night. Charlie's ears still stung from the parting words of his superior that afternoon. "The Feds don't want any kind of interference on this one, Charlie. The Tribal Police will assist, but our office is to stay out unless asked. They appreciate your attending this morning, but that's as far as it goes."

Charlie had known better than to argue with the "Old Man." If there would ever be any chance of moving up into Legal, it would be at his invitation.

Charlie had a pretty good idea of where Lucy Tallwoman's camp was, even from this back way in. He had returned Thomas Begay there several times for some minor infraction or the other, though that had always been from the highway side. He climbed out of the sand wash and into the low cedar hills that gradually rose to a long hogback, bisecting the area. It was beyond this and down the other side where he would find the camp.

This was rough country, and Charlie wasn't used to running up and down these hills as he had as a boy. His grandmother had raised him until he went away to school. Both his parents had been killed when their pickup struck a horse one night while coming back from a Sing near Nageezi trading post. Another truck, coming from the opposite direction, slammed into the wreckage.

There were four people, all Indians, in that other truck, and every one of them survived, though several were badly injured. They had been drinking, and that had probably saved their lives according to the ambulance driver from Farmington. "Indians are better off drunk if they are going to be in a wreck," he said. That was a lonely stretch of road in those days, and no one came upon the accident for several hours. Charlie's grandfather, who had left the Sing somewhat later, arrived just after the police. The state patrolman thought Charlie's parents might have made it as well had they been found earlier. He went on to tell Charlie's grandfather that he didn't think any other kind of human could survive the kind of wrecks he had pulled Indians from. He was an older patrolman and had seen a lot of Indians in wrecks.

Charlie was already sweating by the time he climbed out on top of the hogback and stopped to get his bearings. It had been chilly down below as that's where the coldest air settles after the sun goes down. Up on top it was slightly warmer, and Charlie rested under a large pinyon tree for a few minutes before angling slightly more east to begin working his way off the ridge.

From the top he could see the pinpoint lights of the cars on the highway maybe five miles to the east and knew he was on the right track. He judged it to be about six or seven miles between his truck and Lucy Tallwoman's camp—a long way in this rough country. His people were strong walkers and over the last thousand years or so had become particularly adapted to covering a lot of this type of ground. He had seen people take off walking to a town and not even stop to rest for twelve or fourteen hours, often covering thirty or forty miles in the process. He didn't think this little jaunt would be a problem, even for him.

As the sun finally slipped into the red canyons to the west, he at last edged his way out onto a small rise almost directly above Lucy Tallwoman's camp. Her old blue truck was parked in front of the dwelling, and there was a thin plume of sweet-smelling cedar smoke rising above the mud roof. No one was about that he could detect, though the corral behind the house was filled with sheep, and there was a thin, black horse on a picket rope down in the flats. He waited and watched. There should be a dog somewhere around those sheep, but maybe it was inside with the family or maybe out catching a rabbit for its dinner. Navajo dogs are a self-reliant breed and mostly rustle for themselves. They are not often allowed indoors. Charlie carefully considered these things as he moved through the growing darkness toward the camp. He tried to remember if Thomas Begay was known to have a gun. He didn't think so.

There was the rusted hulk of an abandoned Dodge stock truck at the edge of the yard along with an old wooden buckboard long fallen to ruin. Charlie eased himself down behind the wagon box, a cold sweat starting down his back. He hoped Thomas Begay was not drinking. The cold frame of the .38 felt good under his jacket. He took a measure of confidence from the gun despite his lackluster shooting skill. Thomas had better not try to pull anything funny.

Charlie could see the door of the hogan, pulled shut against the autumn chill. There was no sound other than the quiet chewing and snuffling of the sheep as they settled for the night. It was nearly full dark now, and Charlie was contemplating his next move when a flicker of movement in the cab of the stock truck caught the corner of his eye. In the sudden flare of a match, he could see the wrinkled visage of Lucy Tallwoman's father calmly watching him.

"*Yaa' eh t'eeh*," the old man said softly, only the glow of his cigarette showing in the darkness.

"*Yaa' eh t'eeh*," Charlie responded automatically, trying not to show his surprise.

"Did you come horseback?" the old man asked in Navajo, easing himself down from the truck seat.

Charlie stood up facing the old man. "I wish I had," he said, "but no, there's a pickup truck back there, way back there," and with a rueful smile he waved an arm toward the west.

"Yes, it's a long walk that way," the old man cordially agreed, indicating the direction with pursed lips. Navajos feel it is rude to point directly at something, and most always just indicate directions with their lips or a movement of their head. Charlie had never acquired the habit and once asked his grandmother how so universal a trait had started. She said she thought it must have come from those far off times when one kept his hands on his weapons when giving directions to strangers.

Charlied knew that Navajos, especially old ones, also feel it impolite to be too direct and sometimes take a good deal of time coming to the point in a conversation.

"Well, it's a good night for a walk," the old man observed. "Looks like there'll be a big moon too."

Charlie sighed. He knew this old man's name was Paul T'Sosi, but there again, it would be considered rude to address him by his given name directly to his face—more of the old ways that made no sense to Charlie. It was perfectly fine to refer to a living person by his name—if he were absent—but not within his hearing. It was, however, out of the question to mention the name of a dead person as that might call up his *Chindi* or bad spirit. There were, therefore, specific terms in the Navajo language to cover any conceivable form of personal reference, from distant kinships to the most casual acquaintance. These terms might vary, of course, depending on the person's clan or even if it were a man or woman speaking. It was all very confusing, and Charlie finally decided on the term "Elder Man" or "Distant Uncle." "*Shahastoi,*" he said, "I am sorry to come upon you like this in the night, but a bad thing has happened, and I must speak to Thomas Begay about it." Charlie's Navajo was not so good, but he used it now in deference to the old man, even though he knew Paul T'Sosi spoke English.

The old man studied the end of his cigarette, his face barely discernible in the dim glow. "Thomas has really done it this time, hasn't he?" He said this in English as though anticipating Charlie's thoughts.

"Done what?" Charlie asked sharply. "What has Thomas done?"

"Whatever it is that would bring a councilman ghosting around out here in the dark like a Skinwalker." The old man kept his voice low, but there was an edge to it.

"Is Thomas inside?" Charlie knew it was time for straight talk. "I just want to know what happened up there at the bridge last night. See if we can put this thing together and find out where Thomas really fits."

The old man shrugged his shoulders and moved past Charlie to the door of the hogan. He knew Charlie and Thomas had been friends for a long time. Pushing open the door, he motioned his daughter back down in her chair. Charlie saw the alarm on her face and looked quickly past her to see Thomas Begay sitting on the edge of a bed against the far wall. Thomas, head in his hands, didn't move or show any sign that he noticed them.

Charlie hadn't been in an old-time hogan in years. Even his grandmother had one of the pre-fab government houses. This octagonal hogan was much larger inside than he remembered. The walls were hung all around with Lucy Tallwoman's blankets, each one a serious piece of art. A hissing gas lantern hung from the roof beams, and another smaller one burned brightly above the table against the near wall. There was a sheepherder-style woodstove nearly in the center of the room and two single beds flanking the rear walls. The floor of hard packed clay was swept clean. The room spoke softly of cedar and fresh coffee. Lucy Tallwoman came forward now and motioned Charlie to one of the chairs at the table. *"Yaa' eh t'eeh,"* she said so quietly Charlie could barely make out the words. She brought chipped porcelain cups from a cabinet and poured hot coffee from a tall black pot. She set a can of condensed milk on the table along with a sugar bowl and spoons. Lucy Tallwoman's father sat across from Charlie, shoveling in plenty of sugar before turning his coffee white with canned milk. Charlie did much the same, and Lucy Tallwoman took a place by the stove. No one said anything during this time, and Charlie stirred his coffee nervously, waiting. Finally, it was Thomas Begay who raised his head and looked at Charlie. "You alone, college boy?" He sounded tired.

Charlie nodded. "All alone."

"You come up on us pretty slick for a town boy. I'm going to have to get another dog."

Nodding toward the old man, Charlie said, "I didn't get by him."

The hint of a smile crossed the old man's face as he looked down at his cup.

"Have the police been by?" Charlie asked, watching Lucy Tallwoman as she rose to stand by Thomas Begay. Charlie had never really seen her up close, and he was surprised at how young and good-looking she appeared. No wonder Thomas had stayed on when his wife left, though he expected there was more to it than just good looks.

Thomas Begay ran his hands through his shoulder-length hair. "Tribal boys were here about eleven o'clock this morning, and then, about three this afternoon, they parked a unit in the gully down by the highway. They're still there as far as I know… watching the road."

Charlie grew thoughtful. "They'll be here again late tonight or daylight in the morning."

"That's how I figure it too," Thomas said almost in a whisper, then stronger, "I just came back for the horse and some groceries."

Charlie nodded. "Going to do it the old fashioned way, huh?"

"Well, I was, until you showed up. But I guess you got other plans."

"Plans? No… I don't have any plans." Charlie took a sip of his coffee, deciding to tell them exactly where he was in this thing. "My boss would have my ass if he even thought I'd been out here." He looked from Thomas Begay to Lucy Tallwoman. "I'm not a cop, you know. I work for legal services, and the department head has said hands off." He looked back to Thomas Begay. "The federal agents want you for themselves." He noticed that Thomas wore fresh clothes and had lost the handcuffs.

Thomas smiled. "Oh, I see. You just dropped by for a cup of coffee...for old times' sake...talk about school days, maybe. Well, that's awful good of you. I know it must have been some out of your way, but you really have caught us at a bad time, what with this murder and all." Thomas glanced toward the radio on the box beside the bed. "Seems like that's all there is on the news. Suspect escaped custody...thought to be hiding out on the reservation... Hmmm, must be a Navvyho," he added, imitating Deputy Dudd Schott's nasal twang. And then more seriously, "I'm surprised they haven't called me by name."

Charlie was glad to see Thomas hadn't lost his sense of humor. He had been famous for it in high school. "You haven't been formally charged yet...last I heard. But I think you might be. The Federal Government wants to hang this on somebody, fast."

Lucy Tallwoman sat down at this, and Thomas put his arm around her shoulder—an unusual display of affection for a Navajo, Charlie thought.

The old man spoke for the first time. "They say she was a Sioux woman down here from Washington, poking around in tribal affairs. Something about water rights. Probably wanted to see if the Hopi are still stealing us poor Navajos blind—or maybe the other way around. Well, at least they sent an Indian this time...for all the good it did anyone." He got up and started for the door, giving Charlie a long, searching look on the way out. "Since this isn't the real law, I guess I'd better go back outside and watch some more. Let me know when there's something to eat."

At this last remark Lucy Tallwoman rose and quickly busied herself about the stove, embarrassed at her lapse in manners. Nothing was so urgent that food couldn't be offered to a guest.

Thomas Begay moved over to the table and sat down across from Charlie. "Let me get this straight. You don't intend stopping me when I leave?"

"You got it," Charlie said. "Not only will I not try to stop you, but I will probably have to go with you."

Thomas Begay raised his eyebrows at this. "What do you mean?"

"Well, I have this little problem. My truck is dead, back up the wash, so I don't really have a discreet way out of here. Also, it is likely they will run some air surveillance tomorrow. If they do, they will find that truck, and I'm history. I'll be finished with the legal department for good." Charlie hadn't actually thought about this before and was just now beginning to realize what a fool he had been.

Thomas laughed softly, Navajo fashion. "I'm getting the feeling you don't think I killed that woman."

Charlie shook his head. "Never did. Not even a drunk Navajo would kill someone and then lay down to sleep ten feet from the body. And a traditional Navajo who thought he had killed someone wouldn't rest until he had found someone to do a cleansing ceremony—an Enemy Way or maybe even something more powerful: a full Night Chant, maybe." Charlie paused. He didn't know if a Night Chant would be a proper ceremony or not; there were so many of them, each with its own purpose. "Of course there is the matter of the blood the deputy said was on your shirt and those scratches on your face."

Thomas's fingers went to his face, gingerly feeling the scratch marks down one cheek. "I was in the Thunderbird Lounge last night," he conceded sheepishly. "Danny Joe was there with his wife, Becky. You remember, we went to school with her. Anyway, Becky and Danny get into it, and I got caught in the middle. I got a bloody nose and some scratches out of it." He shook his head. "Check it out. There were plenty of witnesses."

Charlie remembered Becky, a spunky little Mud Clan girl from Waterflow. It sounded just like her, though no one he had talked to thought to mention the quarrel. "The Feds should have a new update out in the morning, and hopefully there will be something in there, or in the autopsy report, that will point in some other direction. In the meantime, if you would like to retain a good attorney, I'm available, for a price of course."

"What's the fee, counselor?" Thomas was no stranger to lawyers.

Charlie laughed. "Well, we can start with something to eat for a retainer."

Lucy Tallwoman smiled shyly from the stove. "I hope you still like Navajo food."

~~~~~~

Charlie mopped up the last of his mutton stew with a piece of fry bread and washed it down with strawberry cream soda. It had been a meal much like those he remembered as a boy, right down to the dish of canned tomatoes in the center of the table. Charlie had enjoyed it immensely, matching Thomas Begay bowl for bowl.

Lucy Tallwoman was gathering food into a burlap bag when the old man poked his head into the hogan to tell Thomas his horse was saddled and ready. Thomas rose from the table, wiping his mouth on his sleeve. "I'll have a look at your truck on the way out. From what you've said, it sounds like it might be in the ignition. I've seen it a lot on those older trucks when I was mechanicing, maybe-so we can jumper around it and get you going."

Charlie looked doubtful but arose from the table thanking Lucy Tallwoman for the meal and making some small comment on her fry bread which he saw pleased her. As he turned from the table, his jacket caught on the chair back, pulling the revolver from his waistband. The gun landed in the middle of the floor, spinning a circle on the hard-packed clay. The three of them stood looking at it. Finally, Thomas leaned over and picked it up, holding it to the light. "This is some nice turquoise," he said, examining the grips, and handing it back to Charlie. "I guess you never know when you are going to run into some wild Indians out here on the Res, huh college boy."

Sticking the gun back in his belt, Charlie shrugged, feeling the heat rise to his face. Lucy Tallwoman looked down at the floor.

Charlie stepped outside, allowing Thomas to say his good-byes. He saw the old man standing patiently, holding the horse and staring out across the alkali flats in the moonlight. When he spoke, Charlie was, at first, not sure he was talking to him. "This was my wife's family's camp," the old man said softly. "We been here a long time now. No one ever died in that hogan, so we didn't never have to leave it." He made a forlorn gesture with his hand. "Her mother died in the hospital." He paused for a moment. "I still work a little at the Episcopal mission in town...room and board mostly, so I stay there during the week. They're still trying to convert me, you know. But...I miss it out here. I don't know why neither...there's nothing here really" His voice trailed off in the night breeze sweeping down from the hills. "I had hoped that people would finally accept this thing between Lucy and Thomas...let them alone, maybe...but that won't happen now." The old man looked very small and frail standing there, clinging to the black mare in the vastness of the night. Charlie said nothing as he was still not certain the old man was talking to him.

Finally, the door of the hogan opened, and in the dim wedge of lantern light, Thomas Begay and Lucy Tallwoman stood looking at one another, holding hands a last moment. The old man brought forth the mare, and Thomas came to hang his sack of provisions on the saddle horn, offsetting this with a large canteen of water on the other side. He tied a blanket roll on the back of the cantle and turned grimly to Charlie. "You ready to roll, college boy?" Without waiting for an answer, Thomas nodded to the old man as he took the lead rope. "I'll be back," was all he said. Charlie nodded to the old man and waved good-bye to Lucy Tallwoman still standing in the doorway.

The two Navajos led the horse into the cedar hills, picking their way quietly through the patches of shadow and hurrying across the open places with only an occasional glance at their back trail. Thomas was a strong walker, and Charlie was hard pressed to keep up. He was almost ready to say something when Thomas stopped suddenly, holding up one hand and cocking his head. Instinctively, they both crouched, Charlie straining every nerve, listening, watching, trying to discern the cause of the alarm. Nothing moved in the moonlight that he could see, and no sound came to his ears. Still, Thomas held point, eyes aglitter, frozen in place, staring at a little patch of cedars off to the right. He exhaled with a *whoosh* when a mule-deer doe and half-grown fawn wheeled and bounced off through the trees, kicking loose, small stones at every jump. The mare remained quiet behind them, having known about the deer for some time.

Thomas reached back and unhooked the canteen, offering it to Charlie with an apologetic chuckle. "That old doe had me going there for a minute."

"Yeah, me too," Charlie replied, pretending to have been aware of the doe. "We should be getting close to the truck by now, don't you think?"

"Just over that next rise if it's where you say it is." Thomas's voice showed some doubt. "This country can fool you if you haven't been in it for a while."

Charlie grinned. "You don't think I'm much of an Indian anymore, do you?"

Thomas shrugged. "You were gone a long time. Sometimes a man forgets."

"Some things maybe, but the things you are born knowing don't go away."

"Well, I hope that's true, college boy, because some of those things you may need out here." Thomas took a sip of the water and replaced the canteen on the horse. "There are reasons for the way we Dinè do things—reasons that took a long, long time to work out. You would do well to keep that in mind." Charlie was mulling this over when they topped out the ridge and saw the pickup truck in the moon-washed track of the arroyo below.

With the aid of a flashlight and some old tools from under the seat, Thomas, much to Charlie's amazement, soon had the truck running. "Ignition wire was broken inside the insulation right at the solenoid connector…I've seen it before…tough thing to find until it comes completely apart. I'd get a new end put on it first chance you get." He showed Charlie the wire. Closing the hood with a quiet click, he shook his head. "These damn trucks are no good in this country. You should make 'em give you a Chevy."

~~~~~

Charlie bounced along the dirt road without headlights. The moon was hitting its zenith now, allowing a perfectly good view of the road, though he still occasionally hit a pothole that rattled his teeth. If he could just make it back up onto the highway before needing the lights, he would be home free. There should be very little traffic at this time of night.

Thomas had finally told him his destination and agreed to meet him there the following evening to see what was to be done, if anything. The place was the ruins of an old Anazazi lookout tower about twenty miles, as the crow flies, from Lucy Tallwoman's camp. Thomas Begay and his black mare would have a long, tough ride ahead of them if they intended to get there by daylight. He had not said what his final destination would be but intimated that he would be safe there. Charlie shivered and flipped up the heater lever. He wondered if he himself would have what it took to make a twenty-mile horseback ride across rough country at night. Charlie was nearly to town before he realized his gun was missing.

3

THE CROW

He had slept only a few hours and was still drowsy when he pulled into the parking lot of the Dinè Bikeyah Cafe just down the road from headquarters. Dawn was breaking above the mesas to the east, and as he stood beside his truck, long tendrils of red and gold reached skyward through a delicately peach-colored horizon. No two alike. That's what his grandfather had often said, and it was true. In all the sunrises he had seen in this country, no two had been the same—always different colors, different patterns, different kind of air even. He pulled in great drafts of the crystal autumn morning. It was like champagne, this air, or at least what he thought champagne must be like. He was going to have himself some champagne one of these days.

Near the door of the cafe, he saw Sue Hanagarni's little Datsun pickup wedged in between two oil-field trucks with drilling logos on the side. Not much drilling going on anymore, but there were enough work-over rigs operating to keep some companies afloat. Charlie had rough necked one summer in the Aneth field, and it had been one of the major factors prodding him to finish his education. No fun, the oil field.

Sue was sitting alone in a booth on the far side of the cafe. Spotting him immediately, she waved him over, smiling, pointing at a huge cinnamon bun on a plate in front of her. Charlie smiled back. He had never known such a cheerful girl, always laughing and joking, never seemed to have a care. In high school Sue Hanagarni had been voted "most popular" and was on the cheerleading squad. She was a *Haltsooi*, a "Meadow Clan" girl. Clan affiliation was the first question a Navajo boy and girl pursued when meeting. It could be the determining factor in a relationship. She should have gone to college, Charlie thought. She'd have done well. He couldn't understand why she hadn't married—certainly not for want of opportunity. You wouldn't find a better-looking girl on the reservation, in his opinion.

"Hi there," she said motioning to the chair across from her. "You look terrible." Her eyebrows arched in surprise. "Out on the town last night?"

Charlie grinned. "Yeah, right. Sunday night is my night to howl." He sat down, motioning for the waitress. "Still on your diet, I see."

Sue smiled ruefully at the cinnamon bun. "How about you helping me with this." Then, cutting the roll in two, she put the larger portion on her coffee saucer and slid it across to Charlie, who tore off a piece with his fingers and put it in his mouth.

"I always said you had the best buns in the country." Charlie smiled around bites of the roll.

"And I always said you knew your buns, Charlie." Sue was laughing now as she sipped her coffee. The waitress brought a menu and the coffee pot, filling Charlie's cup without asking.

"How rude," he whispered, watching her walk away. "I was going to have tea."

"I'll bet you were," Sue said, watching Charlie with that old bemused look Charlie remembered from high school.

As she passed him the cream and sugar, her tone became more serious. "I'm sorry about the case yesterday. The boss said he didn't have any choice but to take you off, what with the FBI and all." She looked up, her eyes bright. "He said he thought you did a whale of a job on the report, though. I think he wished you could have followed through." Here she lowered her voice and leaned forward. "And he said he thought it wouldn't be long before you would be moving up in the world!"

Charlie lowered his coffee cup. "Oh, really. He must be thinking of transferring me to Navajo Mountain. That's about as high up as you can get—and about as far off." Suddenly, something clicked in the back of his mind: Navajo Mountain, *Naatsis'aan*, the sacred mountain, most isolated spot on the reservation. That's where Thomas Begay's father was from. Navajo Mountain people were known to be one of the more traditional groups in the tribe. They still practiced witchcraft up there and did things, all manner of things, the old way. Thomas's mother was of the *Ashiihi*, the Salt People Clan. There were a lot of Salt People in that country. They went all the way back to old White Man Killer, who was said to have come there with his family in 1892. Thomas had spent his younger years at Navajo Mountain. He had talked about it in high school. Charlie had forgotten about Navajo Mountain.

Sue, smiling again, shook her head. "You never quit, do you."

"I know where Thomas Begay is," he said evenly, watching her face.

Sue looked at him a long moment. "You're serious, aren't you?"

"You know it," he replied, buttering the last of the roll and stuffing it in his mouth. "And, moreover, I don't think he killed Patsy Greyhorse."

Sue Hanagarni stirred her coffee, not looking up for a moment. "Well, you are a minority of one then because word has it he will be officially charged tomorrow...Murder 1."

"Tomorrow?" Charlie closed his eyes, shaking his head in exasperation. "That's sort of pushing it, don't you think."

"You tell me. You're the lawyer. I'm just a secretary, remember."

"And a damn good one too. I doubt the old man could get along without you. You carry the whole office from what I hear." Charlie was laying it on a little thick, but he was short of time, and Sue was the only one who could help.

She crossed her arms, nodding her head suspiciously. "You want something, don't you Charlie." It was not a question.

At ten o'clock Charlie was back at the Dinè Bikeyah Cafe, drinking coffee and waiting for Sue to show up for her break. She had been right about charges being filed. Thomas had been named on the morning news as the prime suspect. It had not been easy convincing her to make a copy of the FBI update file. Of course the FBI only released information they thought suitable for other agencies. Still, the file should contain the final autopsy report, and hopefully, a few choice tidbits picked up in the bureau computer system. They had to have something stronger than what he had last seen to get the Federal District Attorney's office to issue charges at this stage of the game. Something must have turned up; that is, something other than suspicion of murder, escape from custody, and grand theft auto.

She drove up at exactly ten o'clock and slid the Datsun right up to the front door on the loose gravel. From the high color of her cheeks and the snap of her eyes, Charlie could tell she was flustered—totally out of character for Sue Hanagarni. She carried a large manila envelope and stopped at the door, glancing furtively about for familiar faces. Apparently satisfied, she walked directly to the table and slammed the envelope down in front of him. "The old man nearly caught me with this. He came in early, asking specifically for this report. He looked like he hadn't had any more sleep than you've had. Something's up, Charlie; the tribal chairman has called twice this morning." Her voice was barely above a whisper, but Charlie had no trouble catching the knife-edged implication. "I could lose my job over this…eight years down the tube…you…you asshole."

Charlie sat speechless, staring as she turned on her heel and stomped away. The little truck spun gravel out of the parking lot, tires smoking as they hit the blacktop. All he could think of was, I didn't know you could do that with a Datsun.

~~~~~~

Thomas Begay needed a drink. His head hurt and the insides of his legs were rubbed raw from the old rough-out saddle. He had ridden into the canyon just as the sun was coming up, and not twenty minutes later, a single engine airplane had skimmed the top of the rim, dipping its wings in an obvious effort to look beneath the overhanging sandstone. Thomas and the mare, however, were already well out of sight, watching from the shallow cave at the bottom of the cliff, screened by the cedars and pinyons. Charlie Yazzie had been right—there was air surveillance. Thomas took another long look around the declivity. There was some rubble along the back wall, clearly from an old ruin, well worked over by pothunters. Only one small room was left standing in any semblance of original form. He hoped the pothunters had found what burials there might be, but he knew better. The pothunters never found them all. He had been around Anasazi ruins since he could remember. Still, they made him uneasy. He stared at the dark window in the little stone dwelling as though waiting for someone to appear, someone who had been gone a thousand years now. Thomas was not so superstitious that he wouldn't stay there, however, at least in daylight.

He gathered some weathered cedar twigs, and using some of the stones from the ruin, he soon had a little fire-pit built that would burn the cedar with a clean, smokeless flame. As his coffee pot began to bubble, he dug in the sack of provisions, hoping in some fit of compassion Lucy Tallwoman had taken pity on him and had included a pint of something to drink. Hope to the contrary, he found nothing and at last set himself to the task of frying bacon and straightening out a few slices of the smashed white bread that had been packed underneath. It was cold in the bottom of the canyon, and the sun would not reach him for several hours yet. He pulled one of Lucy Tallwoman's blankets from the mound of gear by the fire, and wrapping himself in its warmth, he drew a deep breath, imagining that he could smell the scent of her in it.

~~~~~~

Lucy Tallwoman and her father were gathering up such things as they could pack in the back of the pickup when the two tribal policemen showed up. They had a white man in a three-piece suit with them. The shorter of the two policemen took the initiative, starting off in Navajo and haranguing them for some minutes in regard to Thomas Begay. He told them how good it would be if they could convince Thomas to come in on his own and not make them launch a full-blown manhunt—which they would surely do if they had to. The policeman concentrated on the old man, thinking him to be the weaker of the two. "Do you know who this is?" he asked importantly, indicating with his lips the man in the suit.

Paul T'Sosi looked the white man over carefully. "A real estate agent?"

"No, goddammit!" the policeman exploded in English, his face flushing a shade darker. "Not a real estate agent. He's an FBI agent." He turned apologetically to the white man. "These old ones are a little hard to get through to, Mr. Davis. He understands...he's just doing this to aggravate me."

The FBI man pursed his lips, smiling slightly. "That's all right, Joe. I don't think we are going to learn anything here." He nodded his head at the old man. "We'll be seeing you again, Mr. T'Sosi. I hope Thomas Begay hasn't gotten you folks into something you'll regret. It's a serious crime to harbor a federal fugitive, you know. You could go to jail."

The old man thought about this for a moment. "I doubt if you would want a seventy-five year old man with a bowel problem in your jail for very long."

As the police unit was pulling out of the yard, Lucy Tallwoman turned to her father. "You don't have a bowel problem."

"Yes, I have." he replied, watching the retreating dust. "Thomas Begay has given me one."

~~~~~~

Charlie drove back to his duplex in the little government housing complex just outside Shiprock. Carefully, he spread the file out on the kitchen table, looking first at the autopsy report. Cause of death was listed as *asphyxiation* or *oxygen deprivation*. Of course the actual blood tests were not back from the state lab yet, and until they were evaluated—something that might take two or three days—there could be no determination of contributing factors, foreign substances in the blood, etc. There were no signs of outward or internal trauma or violence listed. Sexual assault, the report noted, was not indicated. At the end of the discourse, under summation, it was remarked, in a scrawled addendum, that the possibility of death from natural causes could not be ruled out, though circumstances surrounding the discovery of the body made this unlikely. Charlie shook his head over the paper. The autopsy report, in essence, said nothing and left Patsy Greyhorse's death as much a mystery as ever.

Charlie leafed through the remainder of the file, consisting mostly of FBI computer read-outs concerning the victim's background, associates, work history, etc. The report from the tribal police at Window Rock stated that Patsy Greyhorse's motel room had been entered by a person or persons unknown. No sign of forced entry was apparent, but the room had been thoroughly searched and was in a state of disarray with papers and forms strewn about along with personal items of apparel. There was not, however, any sign of a struggle or violence. It was the investigator's opinion that the room had been entered later in the afternoon after Patsy Greyhorse had come and gone. Her bedside travel clock had been inadvertently knocked to the floor and still registered 3 p.m.—several hours after Patsy Greyhorse had been seen leaving the motel. Charlie scanned through the rest of the file but found nothing of interest. The FBI was not famous for its elaboration in re-ports sent out to their fellow law enforcement agencies. He thought he would read it over again more carefully later.

He almost overlooked the remark on the back cover of the file. It was by FBI Agent Robert Davis and noted that Patsy Greyhorse's husband Edmund LaFore would be arriving that very afternoon and would make an official identification of the body at five o'clock. There was no doubt in anyone's mind of course since a picture I.D. had been found on the body, but identification by next of kin was mandatory in such cases. There was a faxed file photo of LaFore showing a rather good-looking, middle-aged man in a jacket and tie. LaFore, obviously Indian, appeared to be a good ten or fifteen years older than Patsy Greyhorse. He was standing in front of some sort of government building, a school possibly or maybe a hospital. The caption read: "Pine Ridge Reservation, South Dakota."

The agent had listed the motel located at the airport. There was only one afternoon flight, and that was the commuter from Albuquerque, due in around four o'clock. Apparently, no one would be meeting the plane.

Charlie was early and seated himself in a window chair with a newspaper. Only a few people were scattered around the waiting area, and when the flight was announced, they seemed quite surprised that it was on time. As the deplaning passengers straggled across the tarmac to the terminal, Charlie had no trouble spotting LaFore, who appeared much as he had in his photograph. He carried an expensive-looking leather suit-bag slung across one shoulder and a matching overnighter in the other hand. Charlie glanced around the waiting room once more but could find no one in uniform or official looking enough to be from one of the agencies. Of course, Charlie himself seldom wore other than Levis and boots. He fell in behind LaFore as he left the waiting area and was not surprised when the man headed for the Aviator Bar and Lounge—a drink wouldn't be out of line under the circumstances.

Charlie took the stool next to him and said, "Mr. LaFore?" offering his hand, "I'm Charlie Yazzie, investigator with the Navajo council. I hate to bother you at a time like this, but I wonder if you could spare a few minutes?" LaFore took Charlie's hand automatically but looked a little nonplussed. "I thought the FBI was handling everything down here," he said doubtfully, as if suddenly unsure. "I talked to an agent Davis last night...I thought he said the FBI."

"Yes sir, I'm sure he did, but I'm with the Navajo Tribal Council. I'm sure you can understand our concern, sir, considering the nature of your wife's work here on the reservation. We were hoping you might be able to clear up a few things for us." While not strictly the truth, Charlie didn't feel this was out of order.

LaFore rubbed his forehead and sighed. "Of course, of course. I'd be happy to help you any way I can. I'm to meet with Davis at five o'clock," he said checking his watch, relieved to have cleared up the confusion. The barmaid, who had been busy stocking the beer cooler, noticed them now and moved lethargically down the bar with a tired look and a bowl of corn chips. "Double Jack, Black, on the rocks," Lafore said. "And a...?" He looked at Charlie.

"Oh...well...You wouldn't happen to have any champagne open would you?" LaFore and the barmaid looked guardedly at one another. Charlie suddenly felt very tired. He pointed at the nearest tap. "Uh...just a beer would be fine," he said. "A beer would be good." The barmaid shook her head as she turned to the overhead glass rack.

"I'm off duty now," Charlie offered, noticing the look on LaFore's face.

LaFore nodded. "Yes, well...how can I help you?"

Charlie had to stop and think a moment. "Well, Mr. LaFore, there seems to be some question of the exact direction your wife's work was taking. I had hoped that you might be able to shed a little more light on where she was headed with her investigation down here."

LaFore's eyes narrowed. "You mean the council wasn't familiar with Patsy's research? I find that a little difficult to believe under the circumstances. She was working quite closely with the tribal chairman's office." LaFore was feeling him out now, testing the water so to speak. He was a little too slick to suit Charlie, too much like agent Davis, in his opinion. The waitress set their drinks down, and Charlie quickly laid a twenty on the bar. He was somewhat dismayed at how little change she brought back. A double Jack, Black, must be a fairly serious drink. Edmund LaFore has expensive taste. LaFore continued, "It appears no one has a copy of the report she was to give to the special meeting of the tribal council on Saturday night. Agent Davis seemed quite concerned about it when he spoke to me last evening."

"Yes Sir, I think the FBI is having a little trouble finding a motive for your wife's death." Charlie poured himself more beer. "You wouldn't have any ideas would you, Mr. LaFore?" LaFore was already halfway through his double, and Charlie could see the hard lines about his mouth starting to relax; his eyes glistened slightly in the dim light of the lounge.

"My wife," LaFore said quietly, "traveled in some pretty high circles, if you know what I mean, Mr. Yazzie." Charlie didn't know, but nodded anyway, hoping not to lose the momentum of the conversation. "In fact, I had to warn her repeatedly to be a little more careful whose toes she stepped on in Washington." LaFore took another drink.

"She wouldn't listen though. I'm a research chemist with the BIA Health Services. That's where I met Patsy five years ago, working on a water project. Brilliant, brilliant woman, but very headstrong for a Sioux. I'm not Sioux myself, you understand." Charlie lifted his eyebrows. "No, I'm a Crow—*Absoraka* to us Indians." LaFore laughed. "Ancient enemy of the Sioux, actually." He raised his glass in mock salute and laughed. "Patsy never let me forget that either." His glass still in the air, LaFore shook the ice to attract the waitress, who immediately began preparing another drink, glancing at Charlie, who waved a negative finger. LaFore had obviously lost his train of thought, but Charlie could see he was starting to loosen up—probably had a couple on the flight coming down.

"Mr. LaFore, what exactly was your wife investigating down here?"

"Ed...Call me Ed...Charlie is it? Well Charlie, Patsy was a sub-committee chairman looking into some recent leases purchased by the Navajo tribe—leases made to obtain water rights for a proposed irrigation project."

Charlie perked up. He had heard rumors of a large irrigation project in the works. Scuttlebutt had it that the tribe had paid an inordinately high price in consideration of supposedly extensive water rights.

LaFore went on, "Patsy caught some minor discrepancies in the paper work when the papers passed through her office. Even though the individual tribes pretty much run their own affairs, the Bureau still keeps a fairly close eye on any outside dealings. Water rights were Patsy's forte, and she was very good at it. Did you know she had a law degree?" Charlie showed his surprise. He must have missed that in the file that morning. "Yes, indeed. University of Wyoming." LaFore's voice carried an undertone of something ugly. Sinister might be the better word—something

Charlie couldn't quite put his finger on. Something about Edmund LaFore was beginning to rankle him, and he looked away as LaFore stirred his fresh drink with a forefinger before tossing it off in one noisy draft. LaFore's face was flushed, and his voice had become rough, the words beginning to slur slightly, falling almost to a whisper as he looked suspiciously around the bar. Charlie had to lean forward to hear. "Has her computer been found?"

"Computer?"

"Yes, a laptop. She kept everything on the computer and transferred files home to our desk unit by modem nearly every evening." LaFore's voice was wavering, and Charlie could feel the emotion, not grief exactly, but something Charlie thought akin to regret or fear or an admixture of the two. "Agent Davis asked me to bring along the program disk. I have it here in my jacket pocket." He reached unsteadily into the pocket of his coat hanging on the back of the stool. "Everything's here from last week." He held the blue computer disc between thumb and forefinger for Charlie to see. Slipping the disk back into his jacket pocket, he rattled the ice cubes in his empty glass in the established cue for service.

Charlie thought it prudent to leave before Davis showed up and stood to say his good-byes. As the waitress brought yet another double, Charlie hurriedly slid his change off the bar, and as he did so, several coins fell with a tinkle to the carpet. He stooped, reaching under LaFore's chair to retrieve them. "It certainly has been nice chatting with you, Ed. I hope to see you again sometime before you leave."

"Not likely," LaFore mumbled. "Not likely…I'm flying out in the morning." He waved Charlie good-bye over his shoulder and sighed deeply as he contemplated his third round.

As Charlie left the terminal building, he noticed dark clouds building in the West. Looked like rain—unusual for the time of year, but it had been happening nearly every afternoon of late. He stopped on the curb for a moment to examine the blue computer disc he held in his hand. He was going to need some help with this one, and he knew exactly who could handle the job.

Getting into his truck, he poked around in the glove box, looking for the official tribal map of the reservation. He had a pretty good idea where Thomas's Anasazi tower was and thought he remembered an abandoned four-wheel-drive road—once used by wood-cutters—that came within a couple of miles of it. He thought he could find Thomas even though it would probably be dark. First, however, he had to run by the post office.

4

The Tower

The watchtower sat on the promontory of a sandstone peninsula, its sheer walls falling almost vertically to Thomas's camp below. Nonetheless, Thomas had to trek up the canyon nearly a quarter mile before finding the little fissure that doubled back to the top. In places, there were handholds cut into the rock, allowing access from one ledge to another. The path was well worn, and Thomas wondered how many trips would be required to make such a trail. He had waited well past sundown before venturing out, and he regretted it now as he groped his way upward in the dark.
He thought the moon would be up by now. He had his doubts about Charlie Yazzie being able to find this place. Charlie, however, had surprised him a couple of times already. Not a bad guy really, a little uppity maybe, but too much schooling had a way of doing that to a man.

On top, there was a chill breeze out of the north, and Thomas was glad he had thought to bring the blanket. A scatter of small pinyon and juniper trees were strung out across the mesa, most of the larger ones having been cut for firewood years ago. Ragged stumps showed here and there as a little half moon began its rise in the East. On its way to the top, the trail meandered back toward the point, and Thomas now found himself quite close to the old stone lookout tower. He could see the cylindrical form of it looming above the rim in the moonlight. He wondered if Charlie was already there—probably not. He had agreed to come only after dark, and it was a good two-mile walk from the nearest road. He worked his way around the front of the tower to a broken place in the wall where he could squeeze inside.

The room was not large, maybe twelve feet across. The tower had once had two stories. The second floor, along with the roof, had long ago fallen through, leaving a pile of rubble. There were no doors or windows and only a few small apertures in the upper walls. Thomas knew the Ancient Ones had reached the top using pole ladders which could be pulled up after them. The entry way would have been an opening in the flat roof where another ladder led to the interior. Thomas suspected the lookouts spent most of their time on the open roof—a lot of trouble for no more warning than it would afford. Of course some people, archaeologists mostly, felt the structures were not watchtowers at all, but rather had some sort of religious significance.

Archaeologists, it seems, often attribute to things they can't explain something ceremonial in nature. Thomas just knew it cut the wind and afforded a place for a little fire that couldn't be seen from the surrounding country. He pulled some sticks from a packrat's nest and soon had a small blaze going, more for company than the little heat it afforded. He sat wrapped in Lucy Tallwoman's good, thick blanket, hoping Charlie might bring a little something to drink when he came. In his pocket was a handful of pinyon nuts he had gathered in front of the cave below. He took out the nuts and laid them in front of the fire on a flat rock to toast, turning them now and then with a little stick. He ate them slowly, savoring the oily goodness. The pinyon trees didn't bear every year, but it did look like this season might bring a bumper crop in the canyon. The cones wouldn't fully open until the first hard frost. He would have to remember to tell Lucy Tallwoman's father about them. The old man favored the pine nuts, even though they gave his few teeth a hard time. Thomas Begay thought a lot of the old man, who he knew only tolerated him, and that just for the sake of his daughter. Maybe when this was all over, he could make more of an effort to gain his respect.

Even though the fire was making little popping and crackling noises, Thomas heard Charlie coming for some time before he appeared at the opening in the wall.

"*Yaa' eh t'eeh*,"Charlie whispered entering the little room, stumbling slightly on the loose rubble at the entrance. "Hope I didn't scare you, sneaking up on you like this."

"No, No," Thomas said seriously, rolling his eyes in the dark. "You didn't scare me. I been hearing you since you got out of your truck."

Charlie laughed. "I brought you something."

"All right!" Thomas said eagerly, reaching for the sack Charlie was holding. Pawing through the bag in the dim light of the fire, Thomas came up with a cheeseburger wrapped in foil and a little fried apple pie in a cardboard envelope. "Nothing to drink, huh?" he asked, not wholly able to cover his disappointment.

"What, you run out of water already!"

"No, I mean to drink, drink."

"Oh, you mean like this," and Charlie pulled a dark green bottle from his mackinaw pocket.

"All right!" Thomas said again. "What is it, a touch of the grape?"

"Yeah, actually it is. It's some champagne. I picked it up at the little crossroads store." He held it up to the firelight so Thomas might better see the label. "I've been wanting to try some for a while and thought now was as good a time as any. The store guy said they don't get much call for it."

"Well, no crap," Thomas said, shaking his head, examining the wired-on plastic stopper. "You're a little strange Charlie...you know that....You're strange."

Thomas finished his cheeseburger and fried pie, washing them down with swigs from the bottle. "Boy, this stuff tastes like vinegar with bubbles in it."

"Yeah, that's kind of what I thought too," Charlie agreed, thoroughly disenchanted. "Probably been sitting on the shelf for years."

"Never buy any champagne with a plastic cork in it," Thomas said with authority.

After Charlie had gone over the events of the day, including his talk with LaFore and the mention of the charges Sue Hanagarni said were to be filed the next day, Thomas sat staring silently into the fire. Charlie picked up the half-empty bottle of champagne and began dribbling it out beside the fire. "This stuff could kill you."

Thomas looked a little sad but didn't try to stop him. "I doubt it would kill me," he said. "I wish I had some of that hard stuff Freddy Chee had Saturday night. That was some real stuff. I been trying to think what it was. Whooee, I must have been really loaded! I barely remember Freddy picking me up...I was hanging onto a parking meter...I remember that...Freddy and his girlfriend stopped and picked me up. Hell, I can't even remember her name. She was in worse shape than me, could barely talk...nice looking though, from what I could see...and dressed kind of fancy too."

Charlie looked up from the fire. "Freddy Chee, isn't he the one they call "Freddy Two Tongues"—the guy that did a little time down at Santa Fe?"

"Yeah, that's the one. He sure has a nice car…brand new too…candy apple red…Oldsmobile, I think."

"Where in the hell would Freddy Chee get a new car?" Charlie was showing some interest now. Freddy Chee had a reputation—right at the top of the "who-to-watch" list down at the office. A self-styled occultist and bully with a couple of assaults with intent that never stuck. Charlie looked at Thomas across the fire. "Nice Friends."

"Yeah, well, he was just a ride, *hastiin*. I had walked downtown from the T-Bird…had a couple of beers." Thomas looked defiantly into the fire. "Freddy offered me a ride, that's all. He and I had a few shots out of…whatever it was. I must have been a goner cause him and I drinking is the last thing I remember until I woke up with the cuffs on." Thomas rubbed his wrists.

"I been meaning to ask you. How'd you get those cuffs off, anyway?"

"Bolt cutters. I keep some in the truck. Never know when you might need to get through a locked gate."

"What time did Freddy pick you up?"

"Oh, probably two…three o'clock maybe. The bars were all closed." Thomas shut his eyes. "You should have heard the stereo in that car. He was playing some kind of ceremonial tape—flutes, drums, chanting…not Navajo…some other kind. It was great. I can still hear it: *Ya he he he, Ya na he he he.*"

Thomas had a good, clear voice, and the chant, there in the Anasazi tower, sent chills down Charlie's back. He wondered how long it had been since those walls had heard singing. Charlie was trying to remember the time of death listed on the coroner's report. It seemed to him that it had been only an hour or two before the discovery of the body. If Freddy Chee had driven Thomas to the bridge after picking him up, he might have seen something. Charlie rose from the fire. "Where can we find Freddy Chee?"

"Freddy Chee? Hell, I don't know," Thomas sighed, shaking his head. "He's not an easy guy to find. His sister lives across the river from the hospital...just under the bluffs to your left before you start up on top. Sometimes he stays out there with her family. I don't think he'll be much help. Freddy don't like the law."

The wind was on the rise outside the stone walls, and a few raindrops splattered around them, bringing the clean smell of wet sage. Both men rose, and Thomas began kicking dirt on the fire. "I'll stay here one more night to see if they really file charges. Then I'm heading north."

"Navajo Mountain...maybe?" Charlie saw the surprise in Thomas's eyes.

"Maybe," Thomas nodded, smiling a little.

"Tomorrow at noon then." Charlie quietly slipped out into the coming storm.

The wind had risen to a hard, steady blow out of the Northwest, lashing the rain before it in stinging sheets. Charlie was chilled to the bone by the time he found the truck. At least Thomas had a good, dry place to sleep.

~~~~~~

When Charlie drove into the duplex's parking area, his headlights immediately picked up FBI Agent Robert Davis's card tacked to his front door. When he pulled it loose, the message on the back read:

Mr. Yazzie,
Would like to speak to you as soon as possible
concerning the Greyhorse investigation.

Charlie had figured LaFore would relay their conversation in the bar to Davis. It would hit the fan now! He could expect a call from the boss for sure. He leafed through the phone book until he came to the *H*'s. Sue was the only Hanagarni listed, and he dialed her number with some misgivings. She answered almost instantly, giving Charlie the impression she had been waiting by the phone. "Hi, Sue, what's happening?" he said as lightly as possible.

"Charlie!" He could hear the concern in her voice and immediately felt the better for it.

"Listen Sue, I'm sorry about yesterday. I wasn't thinking. I hope there wasn't any more problem about the report."

"Is that why you sent me the computer disc to print out? A computer disk implicating high tribal officials in illegal kickbacks!" Sue's voice had a noticeable edge now. "You're bound and determined to get me fired or in jail, aren't you?" Her voice fell to a whisper. "This is something really big, isn't it Charlie?" He could feel her excitement and wondered fleetingly how far he had involved her.

"Really big," he echoed.

"They found Patsy Greyhorse's car last night, Charlie," she paused. "The FBI was keeping it under wraps, but word gets around."

A vague sense of foreboding was on him as he asked,

"Where did they find it?"

"Right there in Farmington. In the rental agency parking lot at the airport...It was a rental." She hesitated slightly. "Thomas Begay's fingerprints were in the car." There were a few moments of silence as he considered what she had said.

Finally, Sue spoke again. "The rental agency lot is only a couple of miles from the La Plata Bridge. They think they have a lock on Thomas Begay. That's why the early charges. It doesn't look good Charlie.

~~~~~~

He waited until after eight-thirty to call the office of agent Davis and hummed along with several minutes of elevator music before the FBI man came on the line.

"Charlie! Yes…Good of you to call back. Charlie, I was wondering if you could drop by the office this morning…at your convenience of course. There's a few things I'd like to talk over. Won't take but a minute." Davis's voice was noncommittal, and Charlie could read no threat in it; the tone, however, left no doubt that the request was on the order of a summons.

Driving into Farmington, Charlie constructed various scenarios which might take place between Davis and himself. He even let himself entertain the notion that the FBI agent might reconsider and let him take part in the investigation. This was pretty farfetched, he knew. But who could say what the FBI might do.

Agent Davis was not a big man as FBI men go and was pleasant enough should one choose to overlook his eyes, which were a little flat and cold in Charlie's view, but he had often thought the same of other white men with blue eyes. Davis smiled thinly as he greeted him in the outer office but wasn't smiling as he seated himself behind the gray-metal government desk. "Charlie, I want you to know we appreciate your interest in the Greyhorse affair, but quite frankly we'd prefer to handle this within the agency." He brought his fingertips together in a little teepee on the desktop and paused as though uncertain as how to continue. "It has come to our attention that you questioned Edmund LaFore yesterday under the auspices of the tribal council." He cleared his throat and looked pointedly at Charlie. "I also might mention our concern about a missing computer disc that LaFore said he showed you." Charlie noticed a glint of light in the glacier-blue eyes. "That computer disc held some very important information, Charlie. Information that, as it turns out, is irreplaceable." Agent Davis toyed with a pair of spectacles on top of the desk— his right eye had been giving him problems, but he refused to wear the glasses as he felt they lessened his image, even to the point of impacting his authority. Charlie started to speak but was cut off with a wave of Davis's hand. "Oh, we sent a man around to LaFore's apartment in Washington to see if we could pull another copy off his computer, but we were too late. Someone had erased the drive. My superiors are very unhappy, Charlie…In fact there has been some talk of a transfer to a less attractive post." He smiled thoughtfully. "Assuming of course that a less attractive post could be found." Davis stared up at the ceiling for a moment and then went on, the hint of a smile still playing about his mouth. "Charlie, I've been here a long time…a very long time…and during that time I've come to know a number of important people on the tribal council, including the chairman himself. He and I go back a long way—have become personal friends actually—even play some golf from time to time. He paused to let this sink in. "I think I could do you some real good, Charlie, should you be inclined to help us out here."

Charlie shifted uncomfortably in his chair. "Mr. Davis, I hope you don't think I…"

Davis waggled a finger back and forth in front of Charlie's nose. "It doesn't really matter what I think, Charlie. I want you to know that. What is important is what *you* think. I would hate to see a young man of your ability and promise stopped cold at the very beginning of his career." Davis narrowed his eyes, his voice taking on a more ominous tone. "And that's why I have not gone to your boss with this matter, Charlie. I knew if there was any way you could help us, you wouldn't hesitate." He paused and leaned forward in his chair. "All of this is just between you and I Charlie...no one else need ever know."

Charlie sat quite still watching Davis, who settled back into his chair and made a little motion with his hands indicating it was Charlie's turn to speak.

"What, exactly, did Mr. LaFore have to say about our conversation?" The lawyer was coming out in Charlie now. He was getting the impression that agent Davis knew a lot less than he let on. He searched for the proper term. "Fishing"—that was the word. Agent Davis was fishing.

"He said very little, actually," Davis conceded. "LaFore had obviously had a few drinks by the time I arrived, so much so in fact that any identification of Patsy Greyhorse's remains would have been invalid, in my opinion. I told him to go to his room and sober up...that he could make the identification in the morning." He raised a finger. "He did, however, insist on telling about meeting you...and the computer disc which he could no longer seem to locate."

"Well, maybe he'll come up with it this morning." Charlie offered with a half-smile. "Probably just misplaced it."

"No, I don't think so, Charlie." Davis stood up and turned to the window where he watched a late October wind pushing some cottonwood leaves around the parking lot. "Edmund LaFore is dead, Charlie." He turned back. "About two a.m. this morning...near as we can figure. Gunshot wound to the head...appears to have been a short-barreled .38 revolver...close range...very messy." He looked down at Charlie, eyes bleak as river ice. "You have a .38 revolver, don't you Charlie?"

5

THE DOG

Lucy Tallwoman's father was alone now in the hogan. He would not go back to the mission. He would stay here at the old place and take care of the sheep until he heard from his daughter, who had left in the battered pickup only hours before, loaded down with things she might need to get by in a remote area like Navajo Mountain. Thomas had insisted she go to his Uncle John Nez's place. The old man had some misgivings, but she was adamant, saying this way Thomas would know where she was and could join her when he was able. The tribal boys would be watching her of course, hoping she would slip up, lead them to Thomas Begay. Lucy Tallwoman was no fool. It would be a cold day when those two tribal bozos could fool his daughter.

She hadn't wanted to leave him there alone. "What if that FBI came back," she asked. "What if he wanted to cause trouble like he said he could do? What then?"

"I'm not scared of those FBI's," the old man said. "Those FBI's aren't so smart as they think they are." He chuckled privately to himself as he thought of agent Davis sneaking around out there in the sagebrush in his real estate agent suit. "Those FBI's..." he smiled, shaking his head. "Besides, someone has to stay here with the sheep."

It was nearly mid-morning before he called up the dog, unlatched the corral gate, and started the hungry sheep toward the cedar breaks. The sheep were thirsty too and lined out in a quick-trotting string behind the Judas goats. Maybe they could find some sparse feed along the washes coming down from the hills. At any rate there would be water in the mud stock tanks up high and possibly some sunflower patches left along the catch basins. They liked sunflowers, those Navajo sheep. The old man took a piece of cold fry bread and a pocket full of Oreos for his lunch. Thomas Begay had taken the canteen, leaving only a plastic soda bottle for water, which he filled from the barrel outside the door. He was too old for this sheep herding without even a horse to ride. This Thomas Begay business was beginning to wear thin. He had never liked Thomas to begin with, though he could see how his good looks and powerful charm would attract first his granddaughter then later her mother. He had told his daughter no good could come of it, but Navajo women have a mind of their own, and nothing he said could overcome Thomas Begay's power over her. Oh, Thomas was a lady-killer all right, but the old man seriously doubted he had killed Patsy Greyhorse. He didn't think Thomas would have the belly for that. He had to admit Thomas could grow on a person. Even he would miss their little weekend talks. That is, when Thomas had been sober enough to talk. In a nation of serious drinkers, Thomas was in a class by himself.

It was past noon when the sheep grazed their way out onto a narrow hogback several miles from the camp. They had found a good bit of forage on the way up, proving to the old man that Thomas Begay had been keeping them too much below in the alkali flats. Of course these sheep didn't need to be fat. They were *Churras*, the old Spanish-type long-wools. His people had kept them for several hundred years now, favoring them for their toughness and special fleece, which wove like no other. They had become rare, however, what with the government improvement programs. It was the old man's opinion that the government would one day improve them right out of existence. They would already have been gone if it hadn't been for the weavers keeping little bands hidden out here and there.

There weren't many weavers left these days. Not many young girls took it up any more; too many other things to take their interest, he thought. There was now a move afoot to provide tribal assistance, more like grants actually, to women who would be interested in learning the craft. It was all part of the resurgence in cultural heritage gaining new favor in the "Navajo Nation" as tribal leaders now referred to the reservation and its people. In the early times it was often the men who had been the weavers —and potters too. Navajo pottery was never considered near the quality of the Pueblo pottery, being a rather plain utility type wear barely suitable for cooking and daily use. The traditional Navajo blanket, however, (or rug as many whites referred to them) were still considered among the finest textiles ever produced by the indigenous peoples.

He took a great deal of pride in the fact that his late wife, Lucy Tallwoman's mother, had been one of the premier weavers on the reservation, turning out masterpieces one after another. Fortunately, Lucy had felt called to follow in her footsteps, and some said she had, of late, surpassed even her mother's work. Authentic, traditionally dyed Navajo blankets were highly sought after and were bringing astronomical prices from collectors. These old-time sheep were the key to the genuine article in his opinion and reason enough to keep them safe and in the family. You couldn't just go out and buy wool like this.

The old man settled himself under a twisted cedar and leaned back against its shaggy, clean-smelling bark. He watched as the dog gathered the full-bellied sheep in a loose bunch where they were content to rest before working their way back to the corrals. From his place on the ridge, he could see a great distance, even down to the little clearing of the hogan and beyond that to the highway. And by turning his head only slightly, he could look to the west and the great wash where Charlie Yazzie had left his truck when he sneaked into their camp.

It was while he was thinking of Charlie Yazzie and what might make a Navajo boy forget his people that he noticed the slightest smudge of dust far up the wash—the old back way into the camp. He shaded his eyes with a thin, wrinkled hand and squinted slightly against the brightness of the autumn afternoon. At first he thought it might be just a small whirlwind—a dust devil—but no, it was something else—a car or, more likely, a truck. He couldn't make out the vehicle, only that it was traveling very slowly, as though to keep the dust to a minimum. The old man smiled. Someone was coming to visit—someone who wanted it to be a surprise.

The old man didn't hurry the sheep, letting them pick their way off the ridge in the lackadaisical manner he liked to refer to as "moseying"—a term he had once heard in a western movie. It was the kind of word that fit well on the Navajo tongue, and lately he found it creeping into his speech even when using his own language. As he moved along, directing the dog here and there to pick up the few stragglers, he rolled the word around on the back of his palate.

He felt good, hardly tired at all. Maybe a little excitement in his life was what he had needed. Whoever was back up the draw should just now be reaching the end of the road. He figured he had a good hour yet, maybe more. Sundown, he thought, should be about right.

As the old man worked his way off the hill behind the camp, the first thing he spotted was the dusty, gray government car parked at the front door. Agent Davis sat on the hood, hands clasped in his lap, watching the sheep pour into the little clearing. The old man waved a signal to the dog, who immediately began ushering the sheep into the corral, finally taking a stance at the open gate. Paul T'Sosi walked through the cloud of dust and powdered sheep manure directly to the car.

"My daughter was afraid you might be back," he chuckled, watching the light green dust of the corrals settle on the agent's three-piece suit.

Agent Davis smiled ruefully. "Yes, well, your daughter is a very smart lady…and a very lucky one too. This morning the Tribal Police made the mistake of letting her get out of sight before following." He shook his head incredulously and drew little circles in the dust of the car. "They never saw her again."

"Oh, that wasn't luck" the old man grinned. "She's always been a tricky one!"

"They radioed ahead to have a car waiting at the junction of the state highway, but she never showed up…Just disappeared, apparently." Agent Davis, too, was grinning now. "How do you suppose she did that?"

"Oh, I imagine she just moseyed down to that first big wash across the road and pulled underneath the culvert until the boys passed her by."

Agent Davis nodded, still grinning. "You know, that's just exactly what she did…the sign was plain as day, once they went back and looked…made the officers feel a little foolish…if you know what I mean." Agent Davis's eyes narrowed, and he was no longer smiling. "Where did she go from there? That's the question."

"An' a damm good one too," the old man clucked. "I never could keep track of that girl, and believe me I've had a lot of practice."

The two men stared at one another until agent Davis sighed. "Do you have any coffee?"

"Yes...Yes, I do," the old man nodded. "I'll put on a pot if you will just pull your car over there among those boulders. There's a brush shelter, a summer hogan. Just pull right up into it...out of sight." With his lips he indicated the place. "I'm expecting some company. They might be more likely to come down if they think I'm alone."

Agent Davis arched his eyebrows and looked from the old man to the hills. "Not Thomas..."

"I don't know who...maybe some other laws." But the old man sounded doubtful, and the FBI man hurried to move his car. When he returned, he saw that Paul T'Sosi had shut the corral gate and was dipping a pot of water from the fifty-five gallon drum beside the hogan. The old man called the dog, and the three of them went in and shut the door. Agent Davis sank wearily into a chair, as the old man busied himself with the woodstove and the business of making coffee. Davis rubbed his right eye, mostly out of habit. It had been giving him fits, and he wished he had pocketed his glasses this morning. He was only a few years from retirement and had hoped his eyes would at least hold out until then. The dog took up a position by the door watching the white man, growling softly now and again to let them know he was on the job.

"That's a nice looking dog." Davis commented.

"Yes, and he's a good one too," the old man acknowledged from the stove. "Most white men think he's a Border collie or some such modern sheep type, but he's not. He's the old-time Navajo dog. My people have had them for hundreds, maybe thousands of years. The archaeologists say we brought them with us when we first came into this country…before we split up with our cousins the Apaches. They say we may even have had them up North in Alaska after we crossed the Bering Straits. Of course they've found some of the same kinds of dogs buried with the Anasazi, so who's to say." As he turned with the coffee pot, the old man noted the surprise on the agent's face. "Oh…years ago I used to work for the digging crews over around Aztec, in the ruins. Those archaeologists think they know a lot about everything." He smiled. "*We* say we have always been here." The old man passed Davis a cup. "Anyways, that's the old kind of dog."

The agent nodded his head, looking now at Paul T'Sosi in a slightly different light. There was more to this old man than met the eye. He could see now where Lucy Tallwoman got her smarts. "You don't think it's the law out there, do you?" he said, giving a little push of his chin towards the ridge behind the hogan.

"I don't know who it is," the old man answered coolly, "but whoever it is must have a pretty good reason for coming all this way." Secretly, Paul T'Sosi couldn't help but be a little bit glad that agent Davis had come. Even though the FBI man appeared to be in his fifties, he was obviously fit and should at least have a gun about him, which might also be to the good. "The dog will let us know, when the time comes," he said, spooning a little extra sugar in his coffee and passing agent Davis the canned milk.

6

NAVAJO MOUNTAIN

Lucy Tallwoman pointed the truck west on Highway 160 toward the 96 cutoff and then County Road 16—taking her north to Navajo Mountain in the far reaches of the reservation. It was a strange place, or so she had always heard, filled with ghosts and ethereal beings who mingled freely with the people there—people who had been in that country a very long time and did not take kindly to outsiders. Thomas was determined, however, that she should go there until some resolution to the situation could be found. His uncle, John Nez, would take her in and keep her from harm, he told her. John Nez was well thought of in that area, and his business would not be talked around.

Among the Navajo it is often an uncle that takes charge of a boy, providing whatever spiritual and practical training he might be capable of. Thomas's Uncle Johnny had always been particularly fond of him. He had felt even more responsible when Thomas's father had taken to drink, and after some rather scandalous behavior, left the reservation for good. Thomas's mother had remarried and moved away, taking Thomas with her. Uncle John had been saddened and had tried to keep in touch with Thomas through the years, but they seldom saw one another anymore.

Lucy Tallwoman would have to gas up at Kayenta. Her father had insisted she carry two additional five-gallon cans, which would have to be filled as well. She was heading into one of the most isolated spots on the reservation, north of the Utah line, where there were few roads and fewer people. She was uneasy as she pushed the old pickup ever farther from Thomas and home. She was worried about her father and did not like leaving him alone to care for the sheep, but there was no help for it now.

The storm clouds were following her, and she knew she would have to beat them to the cutoff before the roads might become too muddy to travel. The truck shuddered slightly now each time she shifted gears. "Clutch slipping," she whispered to herself. It was not the truck's first clutch, and she knew from experience that it would soon be due for a new one. Clutches didn't last long in that country. Most Navajos are familiar with the vagaries of old pickup trucks, and she had an increasingly bad feeling about this one. This was no country for a lone woman to break down in. The rain caught her just as she turned onto the track to the Nez family compound.

John Nez had married twice after he came back from the army. Neither marriage had proven fruitful—or successful. He now lived alone as far as she knew. The road had become greasy and slick, and the old truck wallowed from side to side in the deepening ruts like a boat in a storm. She had almost given up hope of reaching the camp before dark when she came upon the two hogans and brush arbor that made up the Nez compound. The nearby corrals were filled with sheep and goats. A small bunch of horses grazed what little feed there was beyond the dwellings. Two trucks were parked in the small yard, making it barely possible to turn around. Neither truck looked like it had been moved in a while.

Smoke was coming from the chimney, and a large, mixed-breed dog rushed out to challenge her as she pulled up behind the derelict trucks. As the dog began to bark, she saw a woman peering out the barely open door of the nearby hogan. The door closed abruptly as she shut off the engine and prepared to get out. The dog immediately jumped up on the truck and growled, showing his teeth. This dog had been raised to confront strangers, and she suspected he would bite her if he could. She, on the other hand, had been raised to put such a dog in his place. She waited until it again jumped at the door, then flung it open, smacking the dog up side his head and sending him rolling. She followed this by jumping out and rushing toward him, screaming derogatory words in Navajo. This was too much for the dog, which slunk off, shaking his head and whimpering. When she looked up, a man had appeared, standing in front of the hogan, watching with a bemused look on his face. They stood there for a moment, studying each other. "You must be Thomas's woman," he said in Navajo.

How would he know that? There had been no way to contact him before leaving. She raised her eyebrows in surprise, which the man took as an affirmation. "But how did you…" (Maybe these people up here really did have spirit helpers.)

"San Juan County license plates," the man gestured with pursed lips at the truck. "Thomas is the only person I know from down there." He squinted at her through the falling dusk. "I thought you would be older." John Nez didn't pull any punches.

"I'm working on that," she said, which caused him to smile.

"You were a little hard on my dog," he said softly. "It took me a long time to teach him to bite strangers on the ass." Then his expression turned dark. "I been hearing about Thomas on the news." He looked away and then directly at her. "Did he do it?"

"Well, the radio makes it sound like he did. He didn't, but I bet you already knew that." It was beginning to sleet in earnest now, and Lucy Tallwoman was trembling there in the cold.

"Come on inside," he said. "Looks like you're taking a chill. We'll get your things later, after you've had something to eat and some hot coffee."

She grabbed up a small bag off the truck seat and followed John Nez up to the hogan. The dog was peeking around the edge of the corrals as they passed, and he whined, hanging his head as John walked by and gave him a look.

It sounded like there was a gas generator running somewhere. As John Nez opened the door of the hogan, a brilliant shaft of light fell upon the ground, and Lucy Tallwoman could see these people up here might not be as provincial as some made them out to be. They at least had a generator to supply the camp with electricity, which was more than she had in her own place. As they entered the warm, brightly lit interior, Lucy saw there was a modern propane cookstove set along the west wall—unlike her own wood burning, sheepherder stove, with its stovepipe straight through the center of the roof. This hogan had a potbellied wood stove as well, but to one side. The combination of it and the cook stove was making it a little too warm in there, she thought. There was a woman at the stove with her back to them, obviously tending to a meal in progress. This must be the same woman she had seen peering from the doorway earlier. There was a kitchen table in the center of the room with cups, and John Nez indicated one of the four chairs and took another directly across from her. The woman turned from the stove with a coffee pot, and Lucy Tallwoman was astonished to see she was white and about her own age—much younger than John Nez, who she would think to be well past fifty from what Thomas had told her. She was a handsome woman rather than pretty and moved to the table with a confident, even slightly imperious air. She looked directly at Lucy Tallwoman, as white women will do, and said, "I'm Marissa," and waited, coffeepot extended.

Lucy had always been somewhat perplexed by white people and hesitated slightly now, wondering how she should go about explaining herself. John Nez spoke before she could gather her wits and said simply, "This is my nephew's wife from down-country. She has come a long way and is tired and hungry." He said this in English and thought it pretty much covered everything Marissa needed to know. He left it to Lucy Tallwoman to fill in those details she might feel inclined to supply.

"I'm Lucy Tallwoman, wife of Thomas Begay," she said as though that would explain why she was there. She assumed this woman would know all about Thomas from the radio and John Nez. The white woman nodded but gave no other indication of how this information might have struck her.

Lucy looked at Uncle John Nez, who obligingly filled in the information gap with all he thought *she* needed to know about Marissa. "She's an anthropology professor from Seattle," he said, "who came here last year to study the connection between the Athabaskan root language and the Navajo tongue." He offered this with a slight push of his lips toward Marissa, which Lucy saw slightly irritated the woman. John Nez was a remarkably fine looking man for his age, and Lucy could at once see the family resemblance between him and Thomas.

The three of them sat at the table fixing their coffee, John and Lucy taking theirs with milk and sugar—the white woman having hers black. No one spoke. The silence did not bother the two Navajos as they were used to taking their time in a conversation. The white woman, on the other hand, appeared slightly agitated and stirred her coffee vigorously, though she had added no cream or sugar. A lid rattled on one of the pots on the stove, and she jumped up to see to it. Lucy thought it smelled good, and while she could not quite identify it, she felt it might have something to do with beef and onions. She was suddenly ravenous and hoped whatever it was would be done soon.

John turned to her and smiled. "I see you have come prepared to stay awhile," referring, Lucy thought, to her loaded truck. He said this in a manner which implied it would not be a problem. "The other hogan has a bed and stove, and I will bring more firewood tomorrow." He looked across at the white woman, thought for a moment, and went on, "Marissa lived there the first few months after she came, but she stays here with me now." John Nez liked plain talk and seldom minced words, though he said this last part in Navajo, and Lucy doubted Marissa picked up much of it. It was said that some of the old-time traders knew the language—as well as any white could. But Lucy had known several educators and missionaries who had studied the culture and thought themselves fluent, but not one of them actually was. It took about 20 years to really learn the nuances of the tongue, and you had to start when you were born.

Marissa came back to the table with bowls, spoons, and a roll of paper towels, going back for the beef stew and dumplings, which she dished out in large, steaming dippersful. The stew was as good as it smelled. And unlike the rather plain mutton and potato stew she knew, this one had added tomatoes and carrots along with spices she didn't recognize. She wouldn't mind having this recipe; she thought Thomas would like it.

Navajos devote their full attention to their food, and the three of them ate in silence. When they were finished, Lucy Tallwoman rose with Marissa to begin clearing the table and preparing the dishwater in a double sink that drained to the outside. Lucy was happy to see they still heated their dishwater on the stove just as she did at home. She was beginning to understand why there were so many modern conveniences in this camp. Apparently, there were only so many things a white woman would do without. It seemed these Navajo Mountain people might be a little more worldly than Thomas remembered.

John Nez studied the two women across the room and concluded they were much alike in some ways. It would be interesting to see how they would get along in the coming days.

~~~~~~

Thomas Begay was feeling a little weak. He'd had nothing serious to drink in several days, and it was beginning to show. He had spent the morning cutting feed for the black mare with his pocketknife, though his hands shook so badly he once nearly cut himself. He was keeping the mare out of sight under the lip of the overhang. Already this morning, there had been two more search planes flying over the canyon. He had recognized one of the planes as the little, red Cessna 140 belonging to Fish and Game. Apparently, there was no lack of volunteers. The all-out manhunt promised by the Tribal Police must be underway. It would be just a matter of time now until the ground parties began working a grid, though they must know the chances of finding an Indian like Thomas in that country would be slim indeed.

Charlie Yazzie was to meet him there before noon. Thomas glanced at his black, plastic Timex. "Takes a licking and keeps on ticking," he said under his breath. He could do a whole series of commercials on this watch. It was eleven-thirty, and Thomas began gathering his gear and scattering signs of the camp. Charlie was usually punctual if nothing else, and Thomas had no doubt he would be there. Getting through the searchers shouldn't be a problem. Hopefully, Charlie's official truck would be thought part of the search party itself.

Thomas was sweeping fresh sand over the campsite with a cedar branch when he heard rocks rattling on sandstone. "Ha, ten minutes early!" he said, glancing again at the watch. It was Charlie all right, and he was moving fast along the base of the canyon wall, the top of his head bobbing in and out of view in the sagebrush. "*Eh t'eeh*," Thomas called softly, guiding Charlie to the hidden camp.

Charlie dangled a small backpack from its straps and was sweating heavily. "*Eh t'eeh*," he answered breathlessly, nearly falling through the scrub cedars at the entrance to the cave. He looked around, and noticing the small ruin against the back wall, whistled. "You slept with the Old Ones last night, huh?" He grinned.

"More like I set up all night with the Old Ones," Thomas answered, glancing nervously at the little dwelling, shivering slightly in the warm sunlight.

"Hey, you don't look so good, *hastiin*...life on the Owl-Hoot trail getting to you so soon?"

"I need a drink," Thomas said honestly, "a cleansing ceremony, a sweat bath...and maybe a dozen chocolate donuts." He looked miserable but smiled weakly when Charlie dug in the pack and threw him a package of Twinkies.

"Nothing to drink, huh?"

Charlie shook his head. "Not today, *hastiin*. We have work to do." He pulled out an official-looking tan shirt with a Bureau of Land Management patch on one sleeve, a pair of sunglasses, and a plastic baggy containing something black and fuzzy. "Looks like you and I are going to have to team up for a while," he frowned, passing the items to Thomas. "There have been a few unexpected developments."

"Like what?"

"Like Patsy Greyhorse's husband turning up dead this morning...and a computer disc which may point to a conspiracy in the tribal council."

Thomas's head ached. "What the hell are you talking about?"

"I'm talking about the person or persons unknown who really killed Patsy Greyhorse and a scandal big enough to blow the whole tribe apart." Charlie was looking around the camp as he explained what had taken place since he had last seen Thomas. It took a while longer to explain what the implications might be. "We need to find Freddy Chee and have a little talk with him. I've got an idea he might know more about this than you think."

Thomas stood openmouthed, mind whirling. Freddy Chee! He hated the thought of confronting Freddy Chee. Everyone knew Freddy dabbled in witchcraft. Should he feel threatened, Thomas knew he could be counted on to retaliate in the worst possible way. Lucy Tallwoman had a real fear of him and had told Thomas she was afraid he might someday come for her when he was away.

"You'll have to hide your saddle and gear and turn the horse loose," Charlie went on, studying the mare. "She'll probably head for home."

Thomas was staring weakly at Charlie, shaking his head. "You don't know crap about horses."

Hurriedly, they threw all Thomas's things into the little Anasazi room at the back of the cave, and taking the halter off the mare, Thomas waved his arms and popped her on the rear with a pinecone. She clattered off down the canyon as they turned and faced the climb out to the top and the long hike back to Charlie's pickup.

The sun was warming up the canyon, and Thomas's new shirt was soaked with sweat by the time they reached the halfway point. The Fu Man-chu mustache Charlie had brought in the plastic bag kept slipping sideways on Thomas's upper lip. Charlie hadn't had any trouble keeping ahead of Thomas today. They stopped to catch their breath. Looking back down the canyon, they could see the black mare barely visible at the mouth of the big wash. She was beginning her swing southeast towards Lucy Tallwoman's hogan. Charlie looked at Thomas and snorted. "They always go home."

Thomas, scowling darkly, reattached his mustache. "Where'd you get this damn thing, anyway."

"Joke shop in Albuquerque...last summer. I figured I might someday need it for an undercover operation or something."

"That figures," Thomas said, starting to feel better now that the climb and sweat were cleansing his system. There was hope too in what Charlie had said concerning Edward LaFore's death. Surely it had to be apparent to the federal prosecutors that there was something much bigger afoot here than just Thomas Begay. Freddy Chee, now there was something to think about. He might be the one to make things come together all right. The woman in the car Saturday night hadn't been Freddy's girlfriend at all. That woman in the car had been Patsy Greyhorse. But what was a bad actor like Freddy doing mixed up with someone of that caliber? None of it made sense to him. There were too many loose ends.

Once they were in the truck, jouncing along the rutted trail back to the highway, Thomas appeared increasingly uneasy.

"Hey, *hastiin*, lighten up. You're with me now. No one's going to stop us in this truck!" Charlie hoped he was right.

"It's not that," Thomas almost whispered. "We got to be careful of Freddy Chee. He's a witch. He told me so himself. He talks with the *Yei's* and deals with the Skinwalkers…maybe *is* a Skinwalker." He wiped his mouth with the back of his hand. "He's no one to mess with—I'm telling you! He's been sending dreams to me. Bad things too, man! He's a dangerous person."

"I believe he's a bad person all right," Charlie said, glancing sideways at Thomas, "but he's no witch. He's just a man, worse than most, but just a man."

Thomas shook his head. "You don't understand. You've lost the feeling for this sort of thing, but I tell you, Freddy Chee is stronger than both of us."

Charlie knew that witches were a daily part of life for a traditional Navajo and that believing in them could actually give the suspected witch a very real power over the believer. "Look, *hastiin*, I know how you feel about this sort of thing. I know it's important to you, and I can respect that." Charlie swerved the truck to avoid a young jackrabbit who was under the impression he could outrun a pickup truck, and might well have too if the road hadn't suddenly improved. "I tell you what, as soon as we can, we will find a *Hataalii* and have him do a Sing, an Enemy Way or even a Ghost Way ceremony. I'll do it with you. We'll have it for both of us and invite everyone we know. We can have it at your camp. I'll even pay for the sheep and other food."

Charlie thought a minute. "Hey, isn't Lucy Tallwoman's father a medicine man? Maybe he could do it."

Thomas looked thoughtfully at Charlie for a moment. "Singer," he corrected. "A *Hataalii*, in Navajo. He is one, but he won't do it. He don't do that sort of thing anymore…someone died a long time ago, and he gave it up. I think he's been hanging out with those Episcopals too long to do any good anyway."

Charlie could see he was reaching him now. "Well, we'll just see. If the old man won't do it, we'll find someone else. Who knows, maybe it will be good for all of us."

Thomas looked out the window. "A little religion never hurt no one," he said quietly with a meaningful glance at Charlie.

~~~~~~

Charlie and Thomas pulled up at Freddy Chee's sister's hogan a little after three o'clock in the afternoon. They sat there in the truck listening to the absolute quiet. There was no one around, and the only vehicle—a rusty, tan station wagon—obviously hadn't been anywhere in years. The hogan appeared painted against the backdrop of yellow cottonwoods and buckskin-colored bluffs. Overhead, the autumn skies were a brilliant turquoise, belying the threatening band of dark clouds on the western horizon. The air wafted cool and damp from the river bottom, bringing chill prophesy of days to come.

"No one's to home, looks like," Thomas ventured, obviously relieved.

Charlie sat gazing out over the steering wheel, pinching the bridge of his nose with thumb and forefinger. "Maybe, but we better go check anyway." Thomas's obvious fear of

Freddy Chee was beginning to get to Charlie, and a slight shiver ran up his spine as he reached for the door handle.

As they got out of the truck and walked toward the hogan, they could see a woman and two small children laboring up the path from the river with a bucket of water. She was a small, thin woman in a blue velveteen skirt and blouse and her hair in a traditional bun. She was talking to the children and adjusting the little girl's blouse, identical to her own. She was nearly upon them before she looked up, startled. Charlie could see the thought of running cross her mind, but that would be impossible with the youngsters. Her shoulders slumped, and she came on toward them.

"That's Freddy's sister Sally," Thomas whispered.

Charlie raised his hand in greeting. *"Yaa' eh t'eeh."*

"Yaa' eh t'eeh," came the half-hearted reply. She was not a particularly pretty woman, at least not now. Her face was bruised, one eye swollen nearly shut, the corner of her mouth cut and stained with dry blood. The woman looked frightened and unkempt as did the children—a boy and a girl—who hung back and showed the whites of their eyes.

"We're looking for Freddy Chee," Charlie said.

A shadow passed across the woman's face, and she glanced furtively at Thomas before answering. "That Freddy, he's not here now." Her voice was thin and reedy, and she spoke English in such a manner as to remind Charlie of his grandmother. "He's gone early this morning." She was squinting past Charlie at Thomas Begay, an odd look on her face.

Thomas stepped forward and spoke softly in Navajo, tousling the hair of the children and smiling at them. He talked quietly then to the woman but very fast, and Charlie could not follow what was said. The woman answered in the same low, urgent tone of voice, making Charlie strain his ears for some partial understanding. She obviously knew who Thomas was and was not afraid to talk to him, though she peered suspiciously at his mustache, which was once again crooked. She went to the hogan and came back with a briefcase, which she set on the ground and opened for Thomas to see. He rummaged through the contents for a moment, examining one item in particular, then closed the lid and carried it back to where Charlie was waiting. His face was pale and sweat had broken out on his forehead. "Let's go," he muttered, heading for the truck.

Charlie looked from the woman's strained face to Thomas's retreating back. "What the hell's going on?"

Back in the truck, Thomas stared out the windshield at Sally as Charlie started the engine. "Head for my place!" he said. Thomas's face was hard and twisted now. "A white man came to talk to Freddy this morning and gave him some money and this briefcase. She was in the hogan, but the door was open a little, and she could hear them talking. The white man told Freddy that he would have to get to me before the law did. He didn't know anyone was in the hogan. He mentioned Patsy Greyhorse and Freddy's part in taking care of her and Edmond LaFore."

Charlie turned towards Thomas. "What's in the case?"

Thomas stared straight ahead. "A laptop computer and a .38 revolver like yours, but with blood all over it—also a bag of some kind of meds."

"Who was the white man?"

"She didn't know, but she said she would know him if she ever saw him again." He turned to look at Charlie. Thomas was shaking noticeably as he squinted out the window and licked his lips. "Freddy told the white man he thought he knew where to find me or at least someone who would know."

Charlie jerked the truck into reverse and spun out onto the dirt road. Thomas smiled grimly. "After the white man left, Freddy beat her to make sure she wouldn't tell any-one."

Charlie looked surprised. "So, why did she tell you?"

"I used to know her a long time ago before I got mar-ried." Thomas's face softened. "Those are my kids."

7

THE WITCH

Sue Hanagarni was in a quandary. She sat at her desk on autopilot, going through the morning mail and seething inside. Charlie! That knothead. He should have called her back by now. The final autopsy report on Patsy Greyhorse was in, and there were things in it he would definitely want to know. Like what had actually killed her. Certainly not what anyone might have expected. The blood analyses showed traces of cocaine probably from previous recreational use, and high, though not lethal levels of barbiturates at time of death. But that was not what had killed Patsy Greyhorse. What had killed Patsy Greyhorse was a massive injection of a powerful, nearly untraceable drug similar to synthetic curare. The drug, the report noted, blocks the autonomic nervous system, shutting down the respiratory functions, usually causing death by oxygen deprivation or asphyxiation. These were things far beyond Thomas Begay's capabilities, and the prosecutor's office should be able to figure that out very quickly. Charlie might be right about Thomas being innocent!

Already this morning, two council members had been in the office, meeting behind closed doors with the legal staff. Even more significant was the sudden appearance of FBI agent Robert Davis who spent over an hour in private with the council members. Various clerks and secretaries still scurried about in a dither, though no one in the lower ranks seemed to know any details.

Sue dialed Charlie's apartment every twenty minutes and had tried to reach him on the radio several times. She had penciled him in sick on the callboard that morning and hoped he might be in by noon. The blue computer disc, along with the printout, was in an envelope under the front seat of her Datsun. Information on the disc made it clear that the price the tribe had paid for recently purchased water rights was far beyond the purported value. Patsy Greyhorse had caught the discrepancy when the preliminary paper work had crossed her desk in Washington. Her investigation had been very thorough. At the top of the computer list was Tribal Chairman Arthur Ford, then the two council members who had been in the office earlier. The information was meticulously presented. The old "open and shut case," Sue thought. It wasn't hard to see that Patsy had been trained as a lawyer—the report was filled with legalese that would best be left to Charlie's interpretation. Only Charlie would know what to do.

Sue Hanagarni was an enigma even among her own people. She was always the best at whatever she tried. Even in school she had excelled at things her classmates found daunting. Her good looks and scholastic ability made her a shoo-in for one of the annual educational grants or scholarships offered by the tribe. Her counselor told her all she need do was apply, and she could attend nearly any school of her choice. She had the drive and the grades, plus she would have been a favored minority for most universities. But there was more to her story than most knew. Her family had been very poor, even by reservation standards, and both her elderly mother and father had been ill for some years. They were already old when her mother became pregnant with Sue. It had come as quite a shock. The couple had been childless and didn't know quite what to make of a baby so late in life. That did not stop them from being quite proud of her though, and what little they had went to raise her in a manner that would offer the best chance in life. When she graduated from high school, Sue couldn't bear the thought of abandoning them to go off to college. It had been hard enough in high school when she was away at boarding school. At least then they had been more physically able to care for themselves; now their health had declined to the point they could not do without her. If it had not been for Sue's earnings these last few years, they could not have made it at all.

There had been several determined suitors over the years, including Pete Fish right there in the office. Pete seemed a good enough person but was somewhat older than her, and she had just never been interested in him romantically. That didn't discourage Pete Fish; he was constantly bringing her little gifts of candy and sometimes flowers on her birthday. He was well educated, and many thought he might be in line to head the department one day. Already, he owned his own house and a nearly new car. Most of the single women in the office thought he would make a fine catch and couldn't understand why she preferred to hang out with Charlie. Charlie had no money and few prospects as far as anyone could see.

~~~~~~

As they drove west on Highway 64 toward Lucy Tallwoman's camp, Thomas Begay appeared to be on the verge of panic. Even so, Charlie could see he was determined to intercept Freddy Chee, urging Charlie to push the old truck ever faster. Charlie could hear a faint clatter of valves as they roared through the deepening twilight toward Lucy Tallwoman's camp.

"You think he will go in the back way then." Charlie said.

"Yes," Thomas nodded, clenching and unclenching his fists in frustration. "He used to bring me booze the back way when I was herding sheep. Lucy and the old man could never figure out where I was getting it." He smiled nervously, rubbing the side of his face. "That was back when she was still trying to reform me...before she gave up." This seemed to remind him of something. "Boy, could I use a drink right now!"

Yeah...me too," Charlie admitted. He was trying to tune the radio to the five o'clock news program on KENN in Farmington. In his rearview mirror he could see thunderheads building back toward town. His grandmother referred to them as the "too late rain" of autumn, meaning rain that came too late to do any good. They were causing an annoying static on the radio. There was a strong low-pressure front moving in according to the announcer, when they could finally understand him. "Possible heavy showers toward midnight for the entire area," the report concluded. "Man, we're having a hell of a lot of rain for October!"

Thomas turned to scowl at him. "I really don't care to discuss the weather right now." He shook his head in exasperation. "You really don't get it, do you Charlie! We're going up against a Skinwalker...or worse, and you're talking weather."

"What is a 'Skinwalker?' I mean, exactly. They're like werewolves, right! They can change their form, take the shape of animals and so forth...right?" Charlie tried to keep his tone of voice serious, though he couldn't understand how anyone in this day and age could believe in anything as preposterous as werewolves.

Thomas closed his eyes, not bothering to answer. He couldn't explain the *Yeenaaldiooshii* to someone who thinks like a white man. Many years before, when his family still lived at Navajo Mountain and Thomas was yet a boy, there had been a rash of Skinwalkers, witches some called them. Before it was over there were several people dead and one of the family clans banished from the area. Once that sort of thing got started, there was no end to the bad things that could happen. Any Navajo in his right mind had a healthy respect for Skinwalkers. Thomas's Uncle John still lived up there, and while he hadn't seen him in a few years, he remembered his teachings about such things. John Nez knew more about Skinwalkers than most and how to avoid their evil as far as one could. It was said that John Nez was descended from "Old White Man Killer" himself, a man who had wielded much power in the olden times. That meant Thomas carried that same blood; the thought made him nervous.

Thomas had thought it best to come in from the main road to save time and was now carefully watching the highway in the growing dusk. "Pull over at the big wash just before the turnoff to the camp," he told Charlie. "There's a little side track that goes down under the culvert. We can leave the truck there and sneak up the wash nearly to the camp." Thomas shuddered. "Freddy Chee won't come until after dark."

~~~~~~

Freddy Chee was cursing as he picked his way through the scrubby cedars to the west of Lucy Tallwoman's camp. He had been here a number of times but never in the dark. The moon had not yet shown itself, making the way treacherous, finally causing Freddy to bruise his ankle on a hidden outcropping of rock. The throbbing pain only added to the anger already fomenting against Thomas Begay. It had seemed such a brilliant stroke of luck at the time, the chance to implicate Thomas in the murder of Patsy Greyhorse. He had thought it would give the authorities someone to concentrate on, a quick fix for an embarrassing predicament. Who could know that Thomas, in his drunken stupor, would have such resistance to so powerful a drug, but Thomas had always been tough even when they were children. Freddy had looked up to Thomas then. It was only later he realized how much smarter he was than his cousin. That was when he began finding his spirit helpers. Perhaps he should have saved more of the drug for Thomas, but Patsy Greyhorse had been the main concern.

Now, once again, it had been left up to Freddy Chee to remedy a bad situation. Thomas himself might not be at the camp tonight, but someone would. These old-time Navajos would not leave the sheep alone. Someone would have stayed behind to tend to them, and that someone would tell him where Thomas was—one way or the other. He smiled to himself as he thought of the fear Thomas Begay had shown when he had once revealed himself as a *Yeenaaldiooshii*. Well, it was true, he had always had powers, even as a child, and it was only right that he should have the respect of these people. Now, thanks to his work on the Patsy Greyhorse matter, he would also have grateful friends in high places—powerful friends who would not soon forget his help, who he would not let forget his help. And then too, he still had an ace in the hole: Patsy Greyhorse's computer, hidden safely away. Even the white man didn't know he had it. There were people who would pay a great deal for that computer, maybe as much as they had already paid for silencing Patsy Greyhorse. The white man had naturally assumed that she would have it with her, and she did too. Fortunately, Freddy Chee had the fore-sight to be awaiting her arrival in Farmington and had him-self taken the computer from her rental car as she went up-stairs for the meeting.

Those Oldsmobiles were a piece of cake for someone of Freddy's skills. Had Patsy gone through with the deal, he would have had to come clean with the white man under the guise that he was only protecting their interests, which, indeed, he had been (his anyway, as it turns out). The per-son later sent to rifle through Patsy's motel room had come up empty-handed. Well, of course he had. Freddy Chee had been ahead of them on that one. Prison had not been a to-tal waste of time. It had been more like a government fin-ishing school, and Freddy had been an apt pupil. He had taken well to those white boys' wily ways.

It hadn't taken much to figure out that whoever held the computer still held the power, no matter what kind of deal Patsy Greyhorse had cut. He had not known at the time that there was another computer in Washington with the same information on it, not that it mattered now. Someone had gotten to that computer and erased the drive or some such a business—LaFore himself, probably. That Crow was a clever one. You had to give him that much. Of course now no one knew the whereabouts of the disc LaFore had brought with him, so that might be another wild card. In his drunkenness, LaFore had probably lost it. What else could have happened to it? Certainly, he would have had it with him if he expected to be paid.

Things were looking good for Freddy Chee. There could be no slipups this time. Only Thomas Begay could put Freddy and Patsy Greyhorse together the night of the mur-der. Freddy wouldn't be safe until he had silenced Thomas Begay once and for all. The white man himself had said so.

Freddy had been working his evil magic for several days (little secret ceremonies, utilizing a brandy bottle with Thomas's saliva on it). Any bodily secretion would do, and he had been careful to keep the bottle Thomas had drunk from for just such a purpose. He had hoped the spells alone would be enough, and probably they would have been had he been given a little more time. Now, however, the white man was in a hurry. Always these white people were in a hurry. Now, Freddy Chee would have to take things in his own two hands, so to speak.

One thing you could say for the white man: he wouldn't ask someone else to do a job he wasn't prepared to do himself. He had proven that the night he disposed of Edmund LaFore. Served LaFore right too, threatening them from Washington with that computer disc, then trying to raise the ante. Those Crows were a haughty people. Where could that disc be? The white man had been so sure LaFore had it there in the motel room. He thought LaFore was lying about losing it.

Freddy Chee grimaced as he remembered the white man holding the muzzle of the gun to LaFore's head, giving him to the count of five to tell them. LaFore never changed expression or made a sound even when the white man cocked the hammer. Those Crows know how to die, all right. The white man later said he knew by the count of three that LaFore didn't know where the disk was. That white man was no one to fool with. Freddy shivered. He would have to be very, very careful. The white man had given Freddy the gun to dispose of, but Freddy had kept it along with the computer. They were in a safe place now and might come in very handy. Freddy had learned long ago to trust no one and always to have a backup plan.

He reached the overlook above the camp just as a ragged piece of moon edged up over the cedar hills, casting an eerily luminescent glow on the camp below. Clouds were building all around and large drops of rain began to dampen the smell of dust and dry cedars. Freddy Chee kneeled beneath a pinyon tree, listening to the rising wind and studying the camp. This moonlight wouldn't last very long. Soon everything would once again be darkness. It was important that he have every feature of the camp memorized. Lucy Tallwoman's pickup was not there, nor any vehicle other than the dilapidated Dodge stock truck. There were sparks flying from the stovepipe, and the comforting smell of damp wood smoke came and went on the wind. Someone was there all right just as he knew there would be. The soft bleating of the sheep sounded far away, yet he could have thrown a stone amongst them from where he kneeled.

There appeared to be no dog. That wasn't right; he knew they had a dog, a Navajo dog too—the kind that would sneak up on a man like a coyote, never barking until it was too late. Where the hell was that dog? Surely they wouldn't have it inside. He should have brought something for that dog: a little piece of hamburger with some strychnine in it would have been nice. He was getting sloppy. The white man wouldn't like that. The white man was a stickler for details, planning things out, working the odds, leaving no stone unturned, as he liked to say.

The white man had certainly had Patsy Greyhorse's number. He had known she and her husband had expensive tastes and that Patsy traveled in very fast Washington circles. Oh, the white man had known a good many things. Like how much Patsy Greyhorse liked cocaine, and how jealous Edmund LaFore was of her meteoric rise in the BIA. Those things had come in very handy when the time came to deal with Patsy Greyhorse and her husband. She had been offered a quite generous inducement to drop her investigation as soon as it became apparent what she was on to. But she had, obviously, been too long among the whites; their greedy ways had rubbed off on her. She would not settle for the first offer, or the second. That's when Edmund LaFore had entered the picture, negotiating a very handsome figure indeed. It was as good as settled or so everyone thought. Patsy Greyhorse met with them on Saturday afternoon after secretly driving up from Window Rock. Despite her tight schedule, she had been on time, and things had gone well right up until the transfer when she was told only half the money would be given to her, the other half to be paid in person to Edmund LaFore as per his instructions.

The white man had held his temper rather well in Freddy Chee's view, trying to reason with her, pleading with her in fact. But Patsy Greyhorse had become excited then abusive, finally provoking the white man to constrain her by applying some sort of pressure to her neck, causing her to lose consciousness. The white man had considered the situation for only a moment before sending Freddy for a small black bag from his car and had then given her a barbiturate he said would keep her semi-conscious until a more permanent solution could be decided on.

It hadn't taken the white man long to decide Patsy Greyhorse could not be dealt with on a rational basis. Even her husband, Edmund LaFore, on the telephone had agreed they were running out of choices in the matter. Freddy suspected that LaFore was secretly happy with the way things turned out. Patsy Greyhorse had not been the help to his career that he originally thought she might be. She had plenty of connections, for certain, but she used them only to her own advantage, leaving Edmund farther and farther behind. The white man's suggestion that she might also be trying to cut Edmund out of his rightful share of the money was the clincher. Yes, the white man had them both figured out, playing them off against one another from the start. Now they were both out of the way.

Only this matter of Thomas Begay was left to settle. Freddy eased down the hill toward the sheep pen, coming in downwind to avoid the dog. Where was that dog? Would Thomas have taken the dog with him? Who could say what Thomas would do. Clearly, the man didn't have good sense. He did, however, have good taste in women. Freddy licked his lips as he thought of Lucy Tallwoman. He had thought, at one time, that he himself might have a chance with the *To'ahani* clan woman. He had, in fact, spent a lot of time and money cultivating Thomas's good will. He had made several trips out here with a bottle for Thomas on the off chance he might become better acquainted with Lucy Tallwoman. Then Thomas Begay's young wife had left and Freddy was suddenly out of the running. Just as well. Those Near-to-Water clan women were a little too strong-willed, in his opinion. Still, before he had seen her truck was gone, he had hoped to catch her alone out here tonight. Probably only the old man would be here now. But, here again, things seemed to be working out. He shouldn't have much trouble convincing an old man like that to tell him where Thomas was.

8

THE SINGER

Thomas cautiously raised his head above the wall of the wash and peered intently toward the camp. The moon had shown itself between ragged rifts of cloud, enough light for him to see the car hidden in the brush shelter. "Looks like a government license plate to me."

"Government?" Charlie whispered. He could not see over the top as Thomas was standing on the only outcropping elevated enough for this.

"Federal...I think." Thomas wiggled his elbows up over the edge and pulled himself a little higher. "Hard to tell...too dark." If it hadn't been for the moonlight reflecting off the chrome bumper, he would not have noticed the car at all. There was smoke and occasional sparks from the hogan's stovepipe. Whoever drove that car must have the old man inside—or vice versa. Thomas didn't like it. It was a complication they hadn't foreseen—as if waiting for Freddy Chee wasn't problem enough.

Charlie leaned against the bank of the arroyo, waiting for Thomas to move so he might get a look at the situation for himself. What would a government car be doing out here at night, and why was it hidden in the brush shelter. Anyone coming in from the highway would pick it up in their headlights. "Someone must be expecting company the back way in," Charlie said softly.

Thomas slid down off the sandstone ledge. "Yeah, that's the way I figure it too." He rubbed his hands together and turned up the collar of the Levi jacket Charlie had loaned him. Several big drops of rain plopped here and there in the soft sand of the wash. The two Navajos huddled a moment, looking at one another, backs to the sharp bite of wind, each hoping the other might be the first to suggest a course of action.

"Boy," Charlie said, "I wish I had my gun."

"Oh, really. What would you do? Rush 'em?"

Charlie looked up at the fast moving clouds now hiding the moon. "I would just feel better with the gun. That's all."

"Well..." Thomas was reaching behind his back under his shirt. "I have a gun, and it don't make me feel any better." He brought forth Charlie's .38 Smith with the turquoise set grips.

Charlie stared in the gloomy light, frowning. "How'd you come by that?" He held out his hand for the gun. "I thought I'd lost it."

"You did, *hastiin*. It must have fallen out of your belt again when I was fixing your truck. I happened to notice it after you had pulled out." Thomas smiled in the darkness. "I been meaning to give it to you....It just slipped my mind."

"Yeah right. Well, I'm glad I reminded you." Charlie snapped open the cylinder and felt to make sure all four cartridges were still in their chambers. "You didn't fire it, did you?" He ran the tips of his fingers over the primers. "I might need every shot up there. It's a good thing you gave it back."

Thomas grinned. "What makes you think you're any better shot than I am?" He laughed softly. "I didn't see any notches on those grips."

Charlie smiled in spite of himself. He held the revolver back out to Thomas. "You want it?"

"No, thank you. I have enough charges against me already."

Charlie turned serious as he stuck the gun in his belt, stuffing the bottom of his sweatshirt in around it. He didn't want to lose that gun again. It was time to make a move, and Charlie wanted to do it now while Thomas was still in a capable frame of mind. Freddy Chee and his magic had been weighing heavily on him. "Well what's it going to be, Ace? Do we go in doing a war dance or on our bellies like reptiles?"

Thomas gestured up the wash. "There's a little feeder gully that runs almost up to the camp. If we keep our heads down we can get pretty close."

~~~~~~

Agent Davis was on his third cup of coffee. The old man was surprised; not many white men could drink more than one or two cups of his coffee. They had talked quietly for a while and then lapsed into silence, concentrating on the dog which lay before them, eyes closed, one ear cocked toward the door. Whoever it was the old man had seen coming this afternoon should have had plenty of time to reach the camp by now. Probably had, in fact, reached the camp—come downwind for the sake of the dog. That meant it was probably an Indian, maybe waiting for the old man outside. He doubted the agent's car had been spotted. A stranger would have had to move upwind for that, and the dog would have alerted them. No, he was out there beyond the sheep corral somewhere, waiting his chance.

"Seems the dog would have been better outside," the agent ventured quietly.

"Some dogs would have," the old man smiled, "but this dog might have decided to go hunt up a rabbit or check out a whiff of coyote. Not to mention something bad could happen to him out there tonight. I expect he's better off right in here with us." The old man reached down and patted the dog. "Sooner or later whoever is out there will get close enough for him to smell. He'll let us know."

Agent Davis nodded agreement, knowing the old man was likely right. Davis had spent a number of years studying the Navajos and thought he knew a good deal about them; this old man, however, was capable of throwing him a curve. He may not even have seen anyone coming that afternoon. Davis had no sooner thought this than the dog, raising his head slightly, growled low in his throat. The growl trailed off to an anxious whine, and the dog moved closer to the door, cocking his head to one side, his tail ridged and trembling slightly.

Davis rose from his chair, reaching inside his coat, bringing out a short-barreled revolver. The old man held up his hand, cautioning him to move to the back of the room where a blanket hung, partially screening one of the beds.

Paul T'Sosi cried out in Navajo as the door burst open, rolling the dog into a yipping ball beneath his feet and knocking the old man off balance for a moment. Freddy Chee filled the doorway, bathed in the ethereal yellow light of the lantern, steam rising wraith-like from his wet clothes and tangled hair. He stood there letting his eyes adjust to the light of the hogan. A grim smile played about his mouth as he watched Lucy Tallwoman's father gather himself.

"Well, old man, I see you're having a little trouble standing up to Freddy Chee tonight." He said this in Navajo, gesturing with the knife he held in his right hand. "It's about time you and me met. I hear you're a *Hataalii*—or at least used to be. They say you don't have the stomach for it anymore."

The old man stood silently watching Freddy Chee.

"I don't want to make trouble for you or your daughter, but I could if I wanted. Big trouble, the kind even a healer like you couldn't get around." His eyes narrowed and his voice grew softer. "I just need to talk to my old friend Thomas. You know where he's at, don't you? You just tell me where I can find Thomas, and I'll be on my way. Of course if he's not where you say he is, I'll have to work on your daughter. You wouldn't want that, would you?" Freddy still balanced the knife in his right hand and his eyes glittered in the dim light.

"I expect you'd have a hard time finding my daughter." The old man's voice was steady, but Freddy could see something in his eyes and knew he was on the right track.

"Oh, it might take me a little while, but I can find her, and then the same thing might happen to her as happened to that Sioux woman." Freddy smiled at the look on the old man's face. "If I had a little more time, I might even prefer it that way, but as it is, time is short, and I am willing to listen to you and forget about Lucy Tallwoman."

"You killed Patsy Greyhorse," the old man shook his head incredulously, "and put it off on Thomas."

Freddy smiled, moving closer to the old man. "Well, that would be close, I guess. Thomas should have been as dead as the woman, but you know how hard it is to kill a drunk. The important thing now is to fix that mistake." Freddy hoped the old man wouldn't be as stubborn as that Crow LaFore had been. "Where is Thomas?"

"Right behind you," the old man whispered.

Freddy chuckled. He had to hand it to the old man; he was pretty cool—or senile. Killing the old man wouldn't do him any good, but it wouldn't do any harm at this point either. He waved the knife in front of the old man's face.

"That's enough, Freddy!" Freddy whirled to see Thomas Begay standing in the open doorway, gasping for breath, covered with mud, a chunk of stove wood in his hand. Thomas had started running from the arroyo when he saw Freddy burst into the hogan. Charlie had been right behind him, but he wasn't there now. It was just he and Freddy now.

"Well, Well, Well. The old man does know magic after all. Poof!...and here you are." Freddy laughed nervously, fingering the knife, somewhat taken aback, yet determined to capitalize on this unforeseen luck.

Thomas's eyes were wide. "So you did kill Patsy Greyhorse and tried doing the same to me! You bastard."

Freddy was regaining his composure, facing both the old man and Thomas, moving the knife slowly back and forth to cover them.

"Well, Thomas my man, we do what we have to do. The white man said it had to be done, so I did it. It's just as simple as that."

"What white man!" Charlie, also covered in mud, stood behind Thomas now. He had clearly taken a bad fall, his lip was puffed up and a cut over his eye was pumping blood at an alarming rate. "What white man?"

Freddy flinched at the sight of the tribal investigator. How many more were out there? Was the law already on the way? He peered at Charlie in the dim lantern light, a note of fear appearing in his voice. "Look here now, maybe we can talk this over...strike a deal." He looked from one to the other.

"You'll be dealing with me!" Agent Davis stepped from cover, surprising everyone but the old man. "I'll take that knife."

A strange look crossed Freddy's Face as he whirled toward the agent, knife still in hand. The slug from Davis's .38 just missed Freddy's head, instead smashing into the hanging lantern. The muzzle blast from the revolver filled the small space, and the hogan plunged into darkness. Instinctively, Charlie and Thomas crouched down. There was a curse from Freddy Chee, followed by a yelp from the dog. In the general scramble Charlie felt something brush by him in the darkness and thought Thomas was moving to block the open door. For a moment all was silent, no one daring even to breathe as each assessed the situation in his own way. The old man felt his way to a shelf and turned with a flashlight which cast a knifelike beam around the room. Agent Davis was frozen in place, gun at the ready, a strangely detached expression on his face. The light revealed everyone in the room—except Freddy Chee, who had disappeared into thin air. Charlie and Thomas immediately took the old man's light and rushed outside to see what direction Freddy might have taken. The old man moved to find the matches and light the spare lantern. He thought it a bit odd that agent Davis didn't follow the two outside. The dog, peering out from under the table, paused for only a second before making a break through the open doorway to find Thomas and Charlie. The three of them then followed Freddy's tracks far enough to know which direction he was heading. The rain was already beginning to wash away any sign, and they knew there would be no catching up to Freddy this night.

Blood still trickled down the side of Charlie's face, appearing worse for the rain which was falling in earnest now. "Agent Davis is a little quick on the trigger to my way of thinking. I thought we had Freddy pretty well outnumbered, even with the knife."

"Yeah," Thomas grimaced, rubbing his hands together under a drizzle of water from the roof of the brush arbor. "I wasn't too worried since you were right behind me with the gun."

Charlie coughed. "Well, I didn't exactly have the gun...must have dropped it out there when I fell coming out of the gully...but we could've taken him. He was ready to talk...make a deal."

Thomas looked at Charlie. "No gun!" He spat on the ground. "You need to get a holster for that thing, college boy. One with a safety strap on it."

"Hey, it all worked out for the best. Still, I'd like to have heard what Freddy had to say."

"And you'd have thought Davis would've wanted to as well," Thomas added. They stared at one another through the downpour.

Back inside the hogan, the old man had a roaring fire in the sheepherder stove, and water was boiling for fresh coffee. Agent Davis was sitting at the table, making notes in a little book. He shot Thomas a hard look and indicated the chair across from him. "Looks like you got lucky tonight, Begay. But...you're not out of it yet as far as I'm concerned." He switched his gaze to Charlie, his eyes icy blue slits. "And here *you* are again, Yazzie, right in the middle of things." The agent studied Charlie thoughtfully. "I thought we had an agreement."

Charlie held the agent's gaze. "Just taking care of my client's interests...that's all."

"Oh, he's your client now, is he? Well, that's just fine. I'm sure he's in good hands." Davis inspected his fingernails, smiling thinly he stood, brushing off the seat of his trousers. Raising a cautionary finger, he went on. "In light of Chee's statement, and since you're now Thomas Begay's council, I'm temporarily releasing him to your custody this evening. I'll talk to the federal prosecutor in the morning. He'll want you to come in, I'm sure." And here he stopped and looked thoughtfully at them. "I don't want to hear of you two involving yourselves in this case again!"

~~~~~~

As the sound of the agent's car engine faded in the distance, the three Navajos sat without speaking, sipping their coffee, staring out beyond the walls of the hogan, each thinking his own thoughts. Eventually, the old man looked up, studying the two of them. Then clearing his throat, he began to speak Navajo in a low, clear voice.

"There was a time...when I was about your age that I thought I had the calling to be a Singer. Times were hard for the people then. The government had called upon us to cut back the herds—sheep and horses, mostly. We were ruining the land, they said. The government didn't understand about those animals. They didn't know what those animals were all about. The white man had his shiny new cars to be proud of and his houses with many rooms. But those things were of no value to us out here. There were no good roads for cars or electricity or water for fine houses. All we had was our animals. They were...what we had to be proud of. The White's had jobs in town, work to go to, something to fashion their lives around. There were no jobs out here. Our jobs were taking care of our herds. That was how we knew we were somebody." He stopped to let this sink in. "When those animals were gone, more people took to drinking to pass the time, and that brought on all sorts of sickness." The old man paused, seeing once again in his mind's eye how things were. Thomas and Charlie exchanged looks.

"I had an uncle...maybe you've heard of him...Elmore Shining Horse from over around Red Lake." The old man paused. "No? Well, anyway, he was a great Singer in his day. He came to me one time and said he thought I could learn the Night Chant. He was quite old then and knew it was time for someone else to know the songs, and prayers, and sand paintings that go with that ceremony. It's a very long sing, the Night Chant, very complicated, and not many, he told me, would be up to it. But, you see, I had what they call 'photographic memory,' and my uncle said I might become the youngest *Hataalii* ever. Well, being so young, this talk made me feel good, so I took up with him for several years, going around the country and learning all the things you need to know to do this ceremony."

The old man stopped once again, feeling perhaps he was running on or saying too much. Already he had mentioned the name of someone long dead—something he would not ordinarily have done. Thomas and Charlie, however, urged him to continue, and he could see that they had an honest interest in his talk, so he went on.

"Finally, it came time for me to be in charge of a full Night Chant on my own. My old uncle, of course, would be there to help should I forget something. And there would be several helpers as the Night Chant calls for a number of people to act as *Yeiis*, the masked dancers who go as beggars among the crowd. The family who had brought us in to do the healing for their son were not a rich people, but they called on all their relatives to pitch in and help, which, I must tell you, nearly broke the whole bunch. You know the Night Chant is very expensive. Several hundred people may show up to take some measure of good from the healing, and of course these people have to be fed, and there must be wood and water and all for the whole camp...and, as I have already said, the government had taken many of the sheep and goats, so those few that were left were very high priced. Also, the *Yeiis* had to be paid something, and of course my uncle and myself, though I was to get very little of the goods as my uncle was very tight with his money, which I always thought was not right, him being a healer and all. In any case, it took several days for the family to get things together, and by this time their son was very ill, indeed. I told my uncle that we had maybe waited too long, and it looked to me as though this boy was going to die anyway. But my uncle said no, that was not the case, and in any event the healing would benefit a great many people, and that was what was important in those hard times. So I agreed to go on with it, though I must tell you now my heart wasn't in it. That was my big mistake. Anyone who knows can tell you that to be successful in such a thing, you must be in it body and soul." Here the old man's voice turned thin, and his eyes grew flat and lifeless. "On the seventh night of the Sing, there came a great downpour with much thunder and lightning, and the people had to huddle under their wagons or sit in their trucks or just stand around with blankets over their heads in the pouring rain. But no one went away. They had faith in that ceremony and thought some good could still come of it.

In the middle of the last blessing song, the boy died. We had to break everything up then, and by daylight there were only the tracks going off in every direction to show how many people had depended on that Night Chant to restore their *Hozo*."

Charlie and Thomas glanced uncomfortably at one another while the old man, not looking at them, rose from the table and brought the coffee pot, filling their cups. When he spoke again, it was as though someone else was talking, someone much stronger and younger. "All that was many years ago, but I still remember that chant in perfect order.

All these years I have sung the songs to myself when I was alone or with the sheep, and I dreamed the sand paintings just as they were." He raised his gaze to the young men's faces and said earnestly, "I'm thinking I could do that ceremony again now and make it work—work for all of us."

9

THE CHASE

Freddy Chee was cold and wet. He gritted his teeth as he struggled back up the muddy hillside trail that would eventually lead to his truck in the sand wash. He knew he would have to hurry if he was to reach the truck in time to get it out. Even though it was near the headwaters of the drainage, this kind of rain might have already made that impossible.

He had to get far enough away to have time to think—figure out what to do. It was fairly certain that someone would be watching his sister's camp. He would have to leave with only what he had in his truck, which wasn't much. There was money, however, and what gear he had thought he would need; he had figured Thomas might lead him on quite a chase before he caught up with him. Well, Thomas was irrelevant now. The thing now was to save his own skin. He would be the hunted now.

When, finally, Freddy reached the truck, he was relieved to find the water in the wash to be only a few inches deep. He put the truck into four-wheel drive and began working his way back to the highway. He was sure there would be an all-points bulletin out on him soon. It would be a mistake to go out the way he came in. He thought he remembered a gas-field road well before the highway that would take him across the mesa on a parallel course and give him a few more options. He had to find someplace he could lie low, maybe for a long time.

As dawn approached, he found himself crossing a small arroyo he knew could not be too far from the highway. He turned abruptly to the left and up a deep, narrow feeder gully for a hundred yards. He would have to leave the truck there and continue on foot if he was to stand a chance of leaving the area unnoticed.

~~~~~~

A great calm came over Freddy Chee as he climbed up the shoulder of the highway and saw in the distance a stock truck moving his way in the early dawn light. He set his things down beside him and stuck out his thumb. It is the rare Navajo that will not stop for someone along a reservation road, knowing full well it might be a neighbor or even a relative. This driver found neither in Freddy Chee but was happy for the company, nonetheless. He was taking a load of old ewes up to his brother's place near Kayenta. "My brother thinks he can get one more crop of lambs out of these old ewes," he laughed. "He fancies himself quite the sheep farmer." He was an older man and good natured, but Freddy was glad to see that he didn't know him. "You live around here?" the man asked.

"Visiting. My uncle has a little place just back there by the bluffs," he lied. "My truck's being worked on in Kayenta. I just needed a ride into town." Freddy didn't want to start a conversation and turned abruptly to the window to discourage any further questions.

The driver indicated a paper bag on the seat between them and said, "There are some rolls in that sack there if you're hungry." Freddy reached and took one of the rolls without saying anything. He did not look at the man again nor respond to his attempts to draw him out. When they pulled into Kayenta, it was nearly ten o'clock in the morning. The man asked him where he wanted off, and Freddy indicated the Chevron station coming up on their right. He got out of the truck without a word and simply turned and walked away.

The man watched Freddy carry his duffle to the service station. "There is a person whose *hozo* has left him," he whispered to himself.

Freddy knew that his kind of people (those he might likely find refuge with) were not the sort to keep a secret nor be trusted to provide long term sanctuary, but still there was one place left that might work. It would be possible to be there this very night should his luck hold out. He bought a cup of coffee from the machine at the service station and waited outside on the bench by the door. Sooner or later someone would come along who would be headed in exactly the right direction. He was glad he had brought his sheepskin coat from the truck. On this cold, blustery day, when everyone was bundled up much the same, he felt little concern that he might be recognized. A nasty wind was already pushing riffles of sand along the street, though it had only quit raining a few hours ago.

Time dragged on toward late afternoon, and it became increasingly colder. Freddy walked briskly back and forth, swinging his arms to keep warm. Traffic was sparse, and he was thinking of going inside to warm up again when a newer Dodge pickup with a man and a woman inside pulled up to the pumps. Freddy's eyes lit up when he saw the bags of groceries in the back. These people were headed home, and the sticker on the back window made him think this might be who he had been waiting for. The sticker said RAINBOW BRIDGE in large letters on a background picture of the rock formation itself.

~~~~~~

Charlie took Thomas into the federal prosecutor's office early the next morning; true to his word, agent Davis had already spoken with them regarding the information clearing Thomas and making Freddy Chee the prime suspect. He had cautioned them, however, not to release Freddy's name to the press as he didn't want him alarmed enough to flee the reservation entirely.

They had dropped by Davis's office earlier that morning, but he had not been in, according to his secretary. "He's out of pocket right now—not sure when he'll be back," she offered cheerfully. Charlie just left Davis a message saying they had checked in and would get back to him.

By the time Charlie had finished the paperwork and they had taken Thomas's deposition, his name had been cleared to the prosecutors satisfaction at least enough to allow him to remain in Charlie's custody. It was nearly noon, and both men were hungry. They drove to Charlie's place for fresh clothes and to have a bite to eat. Charlie made them a couple of ham sandwiches while Thomas tried on some of Charlie's clothes. As he set the table the phone rang. It was Sue Hanagarni and she sounded distraught. After quickly apprising Charlie of what had transpired since they last talked, she made it clear that she thought the matter went all the way to the top. She told him she would continue to cover for him at the office but was glad his regular days off were coming up. She was about out of excuses. "Be careful out there," she said, and Charlie could tell she meant it. He looked forward to seeing Sue and spending some time together once this mess was cleared up.

"I like ham sandwiches," Thomas declared, coming into the kitchen and pulling out a chair in front of his plate.

Charlie laughed. "Well, that's good 'cause that's about all I have in the house at the moment."

Thomas picked up his sandwich but hesitated a moment before saying, "I really want to thank you...you know...for all you've done for me these past few days. Not many people would have gone out of their way for someone like me."

Charlie nodded. "Yeah, well, I wouldn't be thanking me too soon. This isn't over yet. Freddy Chee is still the odd man out, and the sooner he's found the better for everyone."

Thomas nodded behind a big bite of sandwich. "And I have a feeling that agent Davis is even more determined to find Freddy than we are."

Charlie agreed. "I have a bad feeling about Davis. I think we should take a run out to Freddy's sister's place and have another little talk with her about that white man she mentioned." Both men seemed lost in thought as they finished their lunch.

At daylight that morning before leaving Lucy Tallwoman's place, Charlie back tracked his path of the night before and retrieved his revolver from the mud of the arroyo. It was now lying beside the sink, and he proceeded to hold it under the hot water faucet, flushing mud and debris from it in a dirty, brown torrent.

Thomas watched him while continuing to eat. "Do you really think that's a good idea?" He asked, swallowing the last bite of his sandwich.

"Oh, it'll be fine. The gun shop guy told my aunt that I could store it in a toilet tank. I don't see how a little rinsing off can hurt." He dried the gun with a towel and swung open the cylinder, spinning it a couple of times, causing little droplets of water to go flying off. "Maybe I should take a hair dryer to it. What do you think?"

Thomas tried to see around him at the gun. "You did take the bullets out first, right?"

Charlie half turned. "Of course I took the bullets out…do I look like an idiot! I already washed them." To prove it, he picked up the rounds one by one and started drying them on the towel.

"I hope we don't have to stake our life on that gun down the road," Thomas said quietly.

"Just let me worry about the gun, *hastiin*. What do you want me to do, get a bow and arrows?" Talking to Sue and knowing he would not be able to see her for a while had made him a little grumpy. Charlie finished with the gun and put it in his jacket pocket which had a zipper, which he carefully pulled up.

~~~~~~

Later that afternoon, as they drove back from Freddy's sister's place, Charlie was even more convinced they should find Freddy Chee before agent Davis did. They were lucky to catch her still there, she told Thomas; her cousin was coming for her and the children. She wanted no more to do with her half-brother. Her more detailed description made it fairly obvious who the white man was. With that as a given, agent Davis would have good reason for finding Freddy first. Agent Davis might take better aim next time.

The briefcase containing the laptop and other evidence was still under the seat of Charlie's truck, but he couldn't quite bring himself to hand it over to any of the authorities currently involved. He certainly wouldn't give it to agent Davis, and he seriously doubted it would be safe with tribal officials from what Sue had told him. He would just have to hang on to it until things sorted themselves out.

Thomas, for his part, was still wary of Freddy Chee, but their recent encounter had strengthened his resolve at least enough that he thought Charlie should know a piece of information he had not thought to mention previously. He didn't see how it could be of any importance but thought Charlie should know. The sun was making a futile last stand against the encroaching night, shooting faint flairs of pink and magenta at the darkening sky. Thomas turned to Charlie and said, "I'm not sure if you ever knew it, but Freddy Chee and me are cousins. His father and mine were half-brothers. Uncle Johnny was the third and youngest brother." Thomas looked over to see how he would react.

Charlie stared straight ahead at the road for a moment while he digested this news. "So you and Freddy were kids together?"

"Pretty much, at least until high school when my mom moved over to Blanco Canyon with her new husband, and they transferred me to the same government dormitories that you and Sue were in. I hadn't seen Freddy again until about a year ago…when he got out of the pen."

Charlie looked over at Thomas and, cocking his head to one side, asked, "So, does Freddy have any relations left up in that country?"

Thomas pondered this. He really hadn't thought about it in years. "Well, no one has seen his dad in twenty years, and his mother…last I heard, was in a hospital or nursing home in Tuba city. Totally lost her mind from what I hear." He frowned. "My dad drank himself to death when I was still in high school. I guess just my Uncle Johnny and a couple of distant cousins is all he's got left up at Navajo Mountain."

Charlie jerked bolt upright in the driver's seat and threw Thomas an incredulous look. "Navajo Mountain?…But that's where you sent Lucy?"

"Aww, Freddy wouldn't go back up there." Thomas stared out the side window into the night. "He stole Uncle Johnny's turquoise watch when we were 12 or 13 years old, and John never liked him since then. Freddy was always in trouble after that. The whole clan pretty much disowned him. John wouldn't have anything to do with him now." Thomas said this in the manner of a man who found his own argument unconvincing. A vision of Lucy Tallwoman played about his mind, and he recalled how Freddy Chee used to watch her when he came to see him. She was afraid of Freddy Chee just like he was.

Charlie did not look at Thomas again but said, "I think we better gas up and head that direction! Navajos are like homing pigeons when they get in trouble—they always go back to the place they grew up."

~~~~~~

Lucy Tallwoman felt right at home in the hogan that once housed the white woman Marissa, and while not as nice as her own, it was clean and warmed up nicely with only a small fire in the iron stove. Still, she hoped she wouldn't be here long. There was something odd about Uncle John's relationship with the white woman that made her uneasy. Not that her own relationship with Thomas would be condoned by anyone, either. She had been think-ing a lot about Thomas and listened carefully to the news on the radio each day, but there was nothing new in the re-ports.

That Marissa was a strange one (that could not be de-nied) anyone, white or Indian, would be hard pressed to describe her differently. She was most likely one of those "Indian wannabees," as her father called them, hanging around reservations, caught up in what they perceived to be the "romance" of the indigenous culture. Indians were well aware of these people and their underlying guilt. They often played them to their own advantage; they did not feel guilty about doing this.

Nonetheless, Lucy and Marissa had gotten on well after that first night, and to John Nez's surprise, they spent long hours together cleaning or preparing food or just drinking coffee and talking in low voices around the table. He had been pleasantly surprised when his new niece had brought in a beautiful blanket, woven in the Two Grey Hills fashion. "This is for you," she said without ceremony, presenting him with the blanket as a token of her gratitude for his help. The blanket was more than a "token" in John's eyes as he knew full well the real value of such a thing.

Early each morning a young man would come from a neighboring camp to take the sheep out for the day and would not bring them back until after dark. He was a good herder and took his job seriously. Even though Lucy never saw the boy, she had noticed that first day how well tended the animals appeared. The boy's father ran a large band of sheep just east of them and would be shipping his lambs and cutter ewes in the next few days. John had made a deal with him to take his entire bunch along when the big stock truck came. John was tired of the sheep business; he considered them "woman's work" and intended to try a few cows next season. Those sheep had belonged to his late wife, and he had kept them for that reason. But he had decided sheep were too needy for a man with no wife or children to care for them.

John Nez was a poor mechanic. He had spent several days working on the better of the two pickup trucks parked in front of the hogan. He had been working on it but didn't seem to be making much progress. The other truck, a near clone of the first, provided a good cache of spare parts, which he was substituting one by one, hoping to find the one that would fix the problem. He told Marissa it was only a matter of time until he had one of those trucks running—or both of them ruined. He mentioned more than once how he wished Thomas Begay were there. He remembered Thomas having a remarkable affinity for all things mechanical—a rare quality among his people.

The afternoon after Lucy Tallwoman's arrival, she and Marissa were making dough for fry bread on the kitchen table. The dog barked, and Marissa moved to the little white, framed window to peer out through the lace curtain. "Looks like someone has come for a visit," she said. Lucy thought the way in which she said this sounded almost like a Navajo, speaking English. Leaving her dough making, she went to look past Marissa at the visitor.

John Nez, who had come out from under the hood, wrench still in hand, looked somewhat surprised to have a visitor. He was a tall, slim man in a black cowboy hat, wearing a large silver belt buckle with turquoise on it and a down vest. He began speaking to John in what appeared to be a rather serious manner. Marissa couldn't place the man but thought he could be from farther up country—a man she had once seen John talking to at the Chapter House. He would be distantly related to John if indeed that was him. John Nez seemed to be giving the man his full attention while casting occasional furtive glances at the truck. Another man was left sitting in the passenger side of the visiting truck, but the women could not see much of him from their angle.

Finally, the tall man finished his talk, and they could see John Nez speaking a few words in reply. They watched as the man, looking disappointed, got back in his truck, turning it around in the driveway. John had a very stern look on his face, Lucy thought, as the truck turned to go out. The women could then see its passenger, who had long hair. He was wearing a heavy sheepskin coat, the wool lined collar pulled up tight around his face. They could not, however, discern his features. Lucy was glad she had driven her own truck around behind the hogan to unload it. There would not have been room for that truck to turn around otherwise.

The women talked quietly to each other about the visitor and other small things. Marissa, who spoke a halting, academic version of Navajo, was interested in Lucy's way of doing the things she had been taught growing up. Lucy knew Marissa was surreptitiously studying her speech patterns and trying to pick out "woman words" she could correlate with similar ones in her Athabaskan language project. Lucy didn't mind because she was studying Marissa at the same time. Lucy liked Uncle John Nez and hated to think he might be in over his head with this woman. She wouldn't like to see him hurt. White women were said to have the power to destroy a man should they take a notion.

Navajo women, on the other hand, had little reason to exercise any such power. They pretty much owned all material goods in the society and had little need for subterfuge. A woman had only to set a man's saddle outside the door to be shed of him. Traditionally, a man owned only his horses, saddle, and whatever turquoise jewelry he might have on him at the time. The sheep, the hogan, and even the dog belonged to the women. That's pretty much the way it still was in some parts of the reservation. Lucy smiled to herself. Thomas didn't even have a horse or saddle; the black mare and its saddle belonged to her father. Lucy had come to believe John's previous wife must have died. Uncle John seemed to have the say-so over everything in this camp, but she knew Thomas had mentioned John having a wife at some point.

When John Nez came back inside, he seemed preoccupied and drank the coffee Marissa brought him without comment. He did not appear inclined to talk. The women, busy now with supper, cast curious looks his way but thought better of asking about the visitor. Finally, John looked up from his coffee as though waking from a quick nap. "That was Marlin Bull from up by Rainbow bridge," he said knowing that the women were wondering; visitors were rare out there. "He heard I had an empty place and wanted to know if I could make room for a family member who came in yesterday and had nowhere to stay. That was the guy in the truck. He told Marlin he didn't want to get down until he knew if we had room for him. Said he didn't want to look like he was begging. Marlin said they were full up at his place, and this guy had no place to stay. He thought he might be around for a while. I told Marlin we already had people staying with us and didn't have room, either." John took a last slurp of coffee and frowned. "I already knew who that guy was, though. I recognized him right off. He didn't think I'd know him after all these years...but I did." Lucy brought the coffee pot and was about to fill John's cup when he said, "That guy was my nephew Freddy Chee."

Lucy jerked the pot back, almost splashing John Nez with hot coffee. He glanced up with a surprised look. "What th..." he exclaimed, seeing her alarm. "Do you know Freddy Chee?" He couldn't imagine how that was possible, but Lucy Tallwoman obviously did know him, and was badly frightened.

Lucy, visibly shaken, set the pot down on the table and backed away, wringing her hands under her bread-making apron. No one spoke for a moment, and then Marissa stepped to her side and put her arm around her. "What's wrong? Who is that man to you?"

Lucy pulled away from Marissa. "I need to get my things together. I need to leave here tonight!" Her voice was barely audible.

John was on his feet immediately. "Easy now!...Easy," he said quietly in the way he would calm a frightened horse. "No need to be afraid." He looked Lucy Tallwoman right in the eye. "Freddy doesn't know you're here. He didn't see your truck, and I never mentioned who was visiting. In fact, no one knows you're here. Even the boy who looks after the sheep hasn't seen you." He touched her arm and smiled reassuringly. "I been knowing Freddy a long time. There's no way I would let him stay here. Ever! He must be pretty desperate to even suggest to anyone that I might let him come back. I told him years ago to never show his face in our camp again." John's expression turned grim, and the women could see that he was remembering things from long ago—unpleasant things.

Marissa sat Lucy down at the table and brought her a glass of water. She was somewhat shaken herself. It had been a quiet life here for the last several months, and now she realized that Lucy Tallwoman was about to change all that—a change she was not sure would be to her liking. Later, when Lucy had been persuaded to return to the other hogan, John Nez insisted Marissa stay with her until she was sure Lucy had gathered herself and would not flee in the night. Marissa helped get a fire going in the stove and brought in extra wood. Lucy seemed afraid to go outside by herself, though Marissa knew she was not ordinarily a fearful person.

Lucy explained to them that Thomas had told her about the part Freddy Chee had played the night he had been arrested. Both Lucy and John felt that Freddy Chee was more involved than Thomas thought. Before leaving her alone, Marissa let the dog in, hoping Lucy would feel somewhat more secure with him on guard. The dog had made amends with Lucy and now accorded her more respect than he did the white woman, whom he considered a pushover.

~~~~~~

Charlie didn't refuel at Kayenta as he still had three-quarters of a tank left and thought that would be plenty to reach John Nez's camp. Thomas wasn't as sure but was anxious to reach the camp and Lucy Tallwoman so agreed they could probably make it. Charlie had filled his thermos with coffee and picked up a box of chocolate donuts at the convenience store when they topped off the tank in Shiprock. Charlie knew Thomas favored that particular brand of donuts for their hard, almost plastic-like chocolate coating. "These things will melt in your mouth, but not in your hand," Thomas had said. "And it doesn't matter how old they are either. I left some under the truck seat for two weeks one time, and they still tasted okay to me."

The night was black and cold as they hurtled north on 98, and about midnight it began to rain, quickly turning to snow—those big, heavy flakes that tend to stack up in that country. By the time they turned on 16, it was falling in earnest, and Thomas was nearly hypnotized by the swirling vortex. They had only passed one vehicle since the turn off, and it had barreled past them so fast they couldn't see what it was. "Do you want me to drive?" Thomas asked. "I know the way pretty good from here." He was afraid Charlie might put them off one of the drop-offs he knew were rushing past them in the dark.

Charlie just waggled a finger in reply, but when the pavement turned to gravel, he slowed down. "Just tell me before it's time to turn off to John's place," he murmured.

Without Thomas, Charlie knew he could easily miss the turnoff altogether in this storm.

It was still two hours before daylight when they pulled quietly into the snow-muffled Nez camp. The dog beside Lucy's bed raised his head and looked at the door, then whined softly a time or two before falling silent. Lucy, emotionally exhausted, slept through it.

Charlie and Thomas sat very still in the cab of the truck as the snow began to pile up around them. "There's no need in waking these people up," Thomas said. "It will be daylight soon."

Charlie agreed. "That will be soon enough."

"Donut?" Thomas asked, passing the box.

The two men made themselves as comfortable as possible and settled down to wait for sunup or whatever might pass for sunup in this storm.

Surprisingly, the system had pretty much moved off to the southeast by dawn, and a bold scimitar of sun was trying to slash its way through the last of the grey wool clouds. When Lucy went to let the dog out, the first thing she saw was Charlie's truck, nearly covered in snow. She at first wasn't sure it was them, but as she watched, someone rolled down the window, and she could see it was Charlie. The dog barked and made a mad dash for the truck, sliding to a halt just short of the door. He remembered what had happened the last time he had jumped up on a truck. He stood his ground, growling loudly and putting on a vicious display of teeth. It was enough to keep Charlie in the truck until John Nez came to the door and called the dog off. Charlie stepped down from the truck, stiff and cold. He reached back inside and shook Thomas, who piled out the other door. Thomas smiled and waved at his Uncle Johnny but went running to Lucy. John Nez stood in the doorway in his stocking feet, grinning at the two as they embraced.

He then turned his attention to Charlie, who he knew from Lucy's description and the official truck. He motioned him to come up to the hogan and shook hands as he ushered him inside.

Marissa was already up making coffee and glanced at Charlie when John introduced him. "Must have been pretty cold out there last night," she said, turning to the stove. Like Lucy, Charlie was surprised to see a white woman but hid it well as he'd had a good bit more experience with white people than Lucy.

"It was a bit nippy," he allowed, "but the snow kept us pretty well insulated, I guess." He really didn't know what else to say to a white woman this early in the morning.

It was some minutes later when Thomas and Lucy joined them. Thomas and Marissa exchanged looks, each having been informed regarding the other. Lucy introduced them and explained that Thomas had pretty much been cleared in the Patsy Greyhorse affair and was no longer on the run. She went on to say that it was Freddy Chee who was implicated and under the gun now—that same Freddy Chee that had been in their front yard yesterday.

The three men seated themselves at the table, and the women began trying to put something together for breakfast. Due to the broken truck, John and Marissa had not been to town in some time and were beginning to run low on groceries. Lucy had warned Thomas that indeed Freddy Chee was in the neighborhood, and the talk quickly turned in that direction. Uncle John said, as far as he knew, Freddy was still up in the cluster of camps near Navajo Mountain, possibly at Marlin Bull's camp. "I doubt anyone up there would have taken Freddy anywhere in this storm."

Charlie frowned. "We did see a vehicle going out late last night just after we turned off on 16...couldn't tell much about it, though." The men mulled this over until Thomas went out to the truck and brought back what was left of the donuts. It had been a full dozen, and there were still eight of them left. Thomas seemed quite proud that he hadn't eaten them all.

Charlie declined, saying, "I already had two early this morning."

Marissa also did not have a donut as she thought they really weren't good for a person. "You know," she said, "they put a lot of wax in that chocolate to keep it from melting."

Thomas studied the donut he had just taken a big bite out of. "Yeah, I wondered how they did that. Makes sense though," and took another huge bite. "Maybe we should just call in the tribal boys and let them take care of Freddy," he mumbled through the mouthful. He was still not sure how to go about handling a witch, especially one on home ground.

"I don't know," Charlie ventured. "I'm not so sure those people would give him up to the Tribal Police." He played with his coffee for a moment and then said, "If he gets away this time, we might not find him so easy again."

Uncle John looked at Charlie with a frown. "There are very few people up there who would mind giving up Freddy. No one wants to hide a witch...and a thief. The problem is," he went on, "the only phone is down at the chapter house, and it's nearly as quick to just go up the mountain and have a look for ourselves."

"Also," Charlie noted, almost to himself, "if we bring in the Tribal Police, it might get back to the FBI. Agent Davis would get wind of it. I don't think we want him in the mix just yet. I guess we could take a little run up there and see what's what."

"Charlie's got a gun," Thomas interjected. "At least I think he's still got one." Thomas thought everyone should know about the gun to ease their minds. "He just washed it and the bullets yesterday; it should still work fine if the gun salesman was right."

Uncle John looked at Charlie and frowned. "You washed your gun?"

Charlie sighed. "It's stainless steel, you know," thinking that would explain things. Thomas, he could see, was feeling a lot better now that the pressure was off, and he was reunited with Lucy. Charlie looked at the two men. "I think maybe we should go up there and check it out."

Uncle John thought likewise. "It won't take me long to find him, if he's there."

The three of them finished a rather meager breakfast and loaded up in Charlie's truck for the trip up country. The snow had already begun to melt some, and John Nez thought they could make it okay if they could stay in the ruts. Thomas had insisted they throw one of Lucy's five-gallon gas cans into the truck bed—just in case.

Once out on 16 they immediately noticed that no new tracks had been made after the snow quit early that morning. Charlie's truck plowed along quite well for the first three or four miles but then began running into drifts that increasingly threatened to be too much for it. Finally, on a steep uphill grade, they lurched to a stop, and Uncle John judged the going would only get worse. They sat there for a while, pondering the situation. "How much farther is it to Marlin Bull's?" Charlie asked, wondering about the possibility of continuing on foot.

"A hell of a lot further than I would want to walk in this much snow," Thomas declared. Uncle John agreed, and they were about to try backing up to find a place to turn around, when the faint roar of an engine came to them from up the mountain. Charlie cocked his head at the noise. "Looks like someone might be making it out this morning."

Uncle John got out of the truck the better to hear. "Yes, it's a bunch easier to come down this grade in the snow than go up." No one could dispute that logic, and soon all three were standing in front of Charlie's truck, waiting to see who might be coming.

The sound of grinding gears and laboring engine increased until the hood of a crew-cab dually topped out a rise in the distance. "That's Marlin Bull's truck," John murmured, shading his eyes from the glare. Charlie unzipped his jacket pocket and put his hand on the .38. If Freddy was in that truck, he wanted to be ready.

As the big flatbed struggled closer, Charlie could see that there were three people in the front seat—two of them apparently women. As the truck pulled even, John Nez could see it was Marlin driving and his wife and daughter on the other side. He moved to the open window, asking if Freddy Chee was with them. Marlin seemed surprised at the question but answered straight up that he was not. "Freddy offered old Willie Chee a bottle of hooch and a tank of gas if he would take him down to Kayenta before the storm moved in last night. They left before it got really bad, but I'll bet they had hell before they got there." He gave John Nez a knowing look. "Freddy was whining that he didn't have any friends up here anymore." Marlin shook his head. "Turns out he was right too. I couldn't find a single person who would take him in."

~~~~~~

Back at John Nez's place, Charlie helped Lucy load her truck for the trip back home. Thomas and John got involved with the broken truck, which Thomas soon had spitting and sputtering then catching with a steady rumble. John grinned, clapping Thomas on the back. "I knew you could fix it." John was very proud of Thomas at that moment and waved at everyone, pointing at his nephew and giving the thumbs up.

John and Marissa had decided to take this opportunity to go to town for groceries while they could still caravan with the others in case the truck still had problems. John went to throw the last two bales of hay—hidden under a tarp—to his hungry sheep. The neighbors would come soon to move them down to the Chapter House and the waiting stock truck. Thomas decided to pour one of Lucy's spare cans of gas into Charlie's tank so they wouldn't have to stop and do it on the way down. Marissa was ready with her list about the same time the trucks were loaded, and the three vehicles began mushing their way toward Kayenta.

10

TRAIL'S END

Freddy felt very fortunate to arrive in Kayenta with only a two-hour wait for the early NTS bus to Farmington. He paid the driver for a ticket and moved to the back of the nearly empty bus. The red and grey mesas were losing their soft white cover and were beginning to look a bit ragged and hard in the harsh light of midmorning. As one after another postcard picture sped past the window, Freddy couldn't help but feel a bit alone and not a little vulnerable. The only person he now had to turn to was his sister—and possibly the white man. He was still amazed at how clever Davis had been, purposely missing his shot that night in Lucy Tallwoman's hogan, instead hitting the lantern, allowing Freddy to make his escape. He chuckled now at how he had first thought Davis actually meant to shoot him. That wouldn't have made sense. Agent Davis needed him, and even if he didn't, he still had the upper hand as long as he had the computer and Davis's revolver hidden safely away at his sister's camp. He toyed with the idea of blackmailing Davis for enough money to leave the country entirely, but where would he go?— Mexico? Certainly he could pass for a Mexican and had even picked up some Spanish while in prison. He thought he might be able to get by quite nicely. He was only 29 years old after all—his whole life was ahead of him. There were any number of things he might do should he take a mind. One thing he couldn't do, at least not right away, was to go to his sister's place. They would have an eye on her. And then in a flash of enlightenment he realized: Davis would be the one staking out her camp! He couldn't afford to let anyone else find him! There was no way Davis would allow anyone else to interrogate him before they had a chance to talk. That would explain why there still had been no mention of him on the radio. Davis intended to talk to him first!

The bus had several stops to make before Farmington, and at Dinnehotso a group of schoolchildren and their teacher got on, taking up many of the empty seats. They were on an outing to Shiprock for the day, and their exuberance made Freddy nervous. He had never liked children, especially noisy ones. By the time they reached Mexican Water, he was gritting his teeth and thinking bad thoughts about children in general.

At Teec Nos Pos an older woman got on and worked her way back through the children to an aisle seat across from Freddy. As she took her seat, she looked directly at him for a long moment and hesitated slightly before setting her bag in the window seat. She smelled of coal smoke and hacked deep in her throat as she settled in. Freddy shifted over to his own window seat and looked out as though searching the countryside for some particular feature. Still, he felt the old woman's eyes upon him from time to time and became increasingly nervous that she might know him from somewhere. There was no doubt he was the object of an official search, but there had been no public announcement of his involvement in anything—as far as he knew. But of course he had not heard the newscast last night or this morning either for that matter. Once in Farmington he would have less concern. He considered himself pretty much average looking for an Indian. White people did not generally take the trouble to differentiate between Indians and for the most part seldom bothered to tell one from the other at all. Indians, on the other hand, seldom turned one another in—unless they had a very good reason. Still, this old woman across the aisle seemed to be taking quite an interest in him. He pulled the collar on his coat up closer around his face and kept turned to the window. The roads were still a little icy, and the driver was taking it slow. Already they were behind schedule. When the bus finally pulled into Shiprock, the children piled off first, and then the old woman rose from her seat and, clutching her heavy bag, looked squarely at Freddy. She seemed to give an almost imperceptible nod before turning and slowly making her way off the bus. Freddy turned in his seat, watching her through the black cloud of diesel exhaust as the bus pulled out. She just stood there staring after the bus as though deep in thought.

Freddy had the bus driver let him off at the far edge of town then crossed over to the other side of the road where he started thumbing his way back to his pickup. He had always had a remarkable insight when it came to people who meant him harm. It had only failed him once or twice in his life. He now felt he would be better off in his own truck. Once it was dark, he could skirt Farmington entirely. It took him most of the afternoon to finally reach the truck, but it was just as he had left it in the arroyo. The truck was already muddy from the long trip across the mesa, but he plastered a few handfuls of watery silt across the license plates, making them nearly impossible to read. He was now thinking more clearly. His entire power base was in that briefcase hidden in his sister's hogan. Without that briefcase he was done.

~~~~~~

When Thomas and Lucy arrived back at their camp, Paul T'Sosi was waiting by the corrals, shading his eyes with one hand and speaking to the dog in a low voice, telling him where he thought they should take the sheep that day. He was stalling for time. Some premonition held him there—waiting—for something.

He saw Lucy's old truck just as it turned off the highway and smiled when they pulled up in the yard. His daughter jumped down and immediately gave him a big hug. He could tell she was happy to be back, and though he had never been much of a hugger, he gave her a squeeze in return. He had worried about his daughter a good deal over the last few days and was now glad to have her back all in one piece. Thomas hung back for a moment, then edged over and stood petting the dog.

The old man appeared pleased to see Thomas as well, though he didn't intend to give him the satisfaction of seeing it. "I see you made that little horseback ride all right the other night," indicating the mare grazing down in the flats, who in turn raised her head and looked toward the commotion in the yard. "When she came in, I thought she might have thrown you, but since she didn't have my saddle on, I guessed not." He cocked his head. "You didn't sell that saddle, did you?" He was smiling when he said this, but Thomas could tell he wanted to know where the saddle was.

Thomas laughed. "No, I didn't have time to sell it; I hid it; I'll go get it in the next day or so." He paused. "I found a nice little patch of pinyon nuts over there," he added as an afterthought. "Maybe we can all go over there and gather a few nuts before the packrats get them all."

The old man studied Thomas for a moment. He thought him somehow changed but couldn't quite put his finger on it. He nodded. "That would be good. It has been a long time since we have done that. It's nice to have pinyon nuts to toast in the winter." This was a newer, stronger Thomas and one he thought he might grow to like—in time.

~~~~~~

When Charlie returned to his apartment, he found a phone message from Sue Hanagarni. It just said to get in touch as soon as possible. Charlie was worn out and needed some sleep but punched up her number and leaned against the doorjamb waiting for her to pick up. When she answered, her voice was measured. "Charlie, when did you get back? The old man has been asking about you." She paused as though looking around the office. "They released Freddy Chee's name on the news this morning. He was spotted on a bus headed for Farmington—some woman whose son used to run with him. She said Freddy turned state's evidence against her boy in a car heist last year. She had been in court for the trial and said she knew Freddy all right and no mistake." Charlie could hear Sue switch the phone to her other ear. "It's been a mess here!" She then lowered her voice. "People in and out all morning. Two government agents from out of town are in the big guy's office right now."

"FBI?"

"I don't think so, Charlie. Someone said they might be BIA. They didn't look like FBI to me. One of 'em was kind of fat."

"Has agent Davis called in or dropped by this morning?"

"Not that I know of." There was a long pause. "I thought you and Thomas were square with him."

"Maybe...but I doubt he thinks so."

"Charlie, I gotta go. Those two agents are coming out now. I'll see what I can find out. Bye!"

Charlie's mind was awhirl as he put the phone down. He was still bothered by the fact that he had not yet turned over Freddy Chee's briefcase to someone in authority. He looked out the kitchen window, tapping his fingertips on the counter, thinking only a moment, before picking up the phone and dialing Davis's office. It might be a good idea to see what Davis was up to. The agent still was not in, and Charlie, again, declined to leave a message. He thought he had a pretty good idea why agent Davis was still out of pocket. He was staking out Freddy's sister's place, of course. Davis knew Freddy would be running out of places to hide, and when word came that Freddy was heading for Farmington, it was a no-brainer that he would eventually turn up at his sister's.

He had just about decided to take a quick nap when Sue called back, and before he could say anything, she blurted out, "Charlie, those guys who were in earlier are special investigators with the BIA! They wouldn't say much but did leave me their card and said I should give them a call if there was anything I thought they should know. They were passing those cards out like candy." He could almost hear her smile as she went on, "Pete Fish is running around here like an old lady, telling everyone they should cooperate fully with those agents as our office has nothing to hide!" They both chuckled over that, and Charlie wrote down the motel where he could get in touch with the BIA investigators. He told Sue he had some unfinished business to attend to that afternoon but would meet up with her for breakfast the next morning. Sue sounded happy with that as she hung up.

~~~~~~

Lucy dropped Thomas by Charlie's place that afternoon on her way into town for groceries. Thomas was still in Charlie's custody at least until they heard different from the prosecutor's office. When Charlie told Thomas what he thought about Davis waiting for Freddy at his sister's, Thomas nodded. "I figured that. I'm glad Sally is out of there."

"Are you up for a little trip back out there tonight, *hastiin?*" Freddy wouldn't come until well after dark, but Davis probably figured there was no telling what he would do. It would make sense for Davis to be out there; he would get only one chance at this.

Charlie finally decided they should first take a run by the BIA agent's motel and drop off the briefcase along with LaFore's floppy disk. He would breathe a lot easier when that was in safe hands. It was nearly dark when they left Farmington and crossed to the reservation by way of the old river bridge.

~~~~~~

Thomas thought if they turned off just after the bridge and followed the river upstream, they could stay along the bank and not be seen until nearly to Sally's camp. He ticked off the advantages of this route for Charlie on the fingers of one hand: It was an old stock-drive road, and he felt they would be able to run with their lights off for the last mile or two; there would still be a pretty good moon, and if they went slow, there should be enough light; there would be the noise of the river and the night breeze rustling downstream to cover the sound of their coming!

Charlie looked surprised. "Very well thought out!" Thomas could think quite clearly when sober, and he had been sober now for some days. Charlie thought it was beginning to show.

Thomas was pretty pleased with the plan himself. "I hope Freddy will be as surprised as you seem to be."

As they jounced along the barely discernible track, Charlie could see by the tall grass in the ruts that no one had been this way for some time. The possibility that Davis himself might have come this way had been niggling away at his mind. Davis must be up above at the base of the bluffs. There were several pull-offs just above the camp that would offer a shielded view—that is, if Davis was really out here at all. Charlie had long since come to the conclusion that Freddy and Davis shared one major personality trait: neither of them could be counted on to do the expected. Freddy was pretty easy to figure once you got a bead on him, but Davis was a flier, even for a white man. Who would figure an FBI man to be involved in something like this, which was exactly what allowed him to spin his little web with impunity. In some ways agent Davis was far worse than Freddy. While Freddy had obviously been complicit, it had been Davis who engineered the murders, and Charlie suspected he would not hesitate to kill again should he feel it necessary. At this point, Davis must still think Freddy was the only one that could link him to the murders. Whether Freddy knew it or not, this put him in a very tenuous position, indeed. Freddy's life was on the line this night, and wily though he might be, Charlie wasn't convinced he could out maneuver the FBI man.

Thomas suddenly leaned forward, gripping the truck's dashboard. "Did you hear something?"

"Uh, no, I didn't …like what?"

"I'm not sure…could have been…I don't know…something." Both men listened. "It's about time to turn off the lights anyway. Once we get beyond this bank, someone could see them from the camp."

Charlie switched off the lights and immediately had to reduce his speed to a crawl, just idling along in low gear, making very little noise. They were able to go another mile or so, ghosting along in the eerie glow of the moonlight, eventually nosing up into a small clearing in the brush and turning off the engine. The two men sat silent for a moment. Charlie reached up and removed the bulb from the dome light, then both eased out of the truck and slowly moved up the road side by side.

Thomas touched Charlie's arm and whispered, "You still got the gun?"

Charlie grimaced at him and nodded, touching his jacket pocket and holding up a thumb. He could see Thomas was frightened but mainly just of Freddy. Agent Davis really didn't seem to bother him at all. He should have told Thomas the gun was loaded with silver bullets.

At the edge of the clearing, they could see the entire camp and immediately noticed Freddy Chee's truck parked to the side and slightly behind the hogan. Freddy was here alright! They moved up behind the hulk of the abandoned station wagon parked at the side of the yard and crouched there, considering their next move. Charlie unzipped his jacket pocket and pulled out the gun, checking the cylinder, reassuring himself that it was indeed still loaded. It crossed his mind that he might never have to fire these four rounds—ever. He might someday be able to show them to his grandchildren and explain to them what an exciting life these bullets had once led. He could see that Thomas took a good measure of confidence from the gun and was glad he had it on that account alone. He hoped he wouldn't be called upon to use it as he was not entirely sure he was up to shooting anyone. The relatives who bought him the gun would be disappointed.

The hogan appeared dark. The moon had disappeared, leaving only a glimmer of light. Thomas nudged Charlie and moved to the front of the old car, staying low and watching where he put his feet. He hoped Charlie would follow suit and try not to stumble or fall over. They both paused, and raising their heads slightly, peered all around in the darkness, trying to discern the slightest thing that might be out of place. Charlie had a hard time believing Freddy wasn't waiting in there in the dark. He gave Thomas's jacket a tug, indicating he would now take the lead, holding the gun up slightly and raising his eyebrows in such a manner that Thomas might take courage and remain strong in what was to come. Finally, the two jumped up and on cue rushed the hogan. Charlie reached the dwelling first and gave a mighty kick at the heavy cottonwood door. It didn't budge, and Charlie hopped silently on one foot as Thomas reached around and lifted the latch, allowing the door to swing open. It was pitch black in the hogan, and Thomas was glad he had brought the flashlight from the glove box of Charlie's truck. He quickly switched it on, playing the beam around the room. At first, they saw nothing out of the ordinary, and Thomas was about to give a sigh of relief, but as he lowered the light to show their way in, they nearly stepped on Freddy Chee.

"Woo-ha!" Thomas exclaimed, jumping back, allowing Charlie a clear shot should one be required.

Charlie, teeth clenched, gun at the ready, was paralyzed at the sight of Freddy lying there, staring sightlessly into the dark, a twisted grin distorting his features and one hand held out like a claw in front of him. He had two rather obvious holes in his chest and had probably died quickly but not before pumping out an impressive pool of blood. As they stared in horror, Thomas quickly realized Freddy Chee was no longer a determining factor in his life and quickly backed out of the hogan lest Freddy's *chindi* descend upon him from the pole ceiling and take up where Freddy had left off.

Charlie quickly regained his senses, and as he turned to follow Thomas, the entire camp was emblazoned in a brilliant white light. A car had rolled silently and in darkness down the hill, catching both men unaware. They stood there transfixed in the doorway, shielding their eyes against the glare. Thomas could make out a dark figure move between the headlights.

"Hold it right there, the both of you!" commanded a loud voice, which they both instantly recognized as agent Davis.

"I have warned the two of you repeatedly to stay out of this affair. And now, it appears you've murdered poor Mr. Chee."

There was a grim hint of humor in the agent's voice, and Charlie wasn't sure if he was serious or not.

Charlie was still standing slightly behind Thomas, gun at his side, when a shot blasted out, and a slug slammed into the cedar doorpost next to his head. A second shot exploded, and Thomas gave a yelp and twisted sideways. Charlie, instantly and without thinking, threw up his revolver and emptied all four rounds into the space between the headlights. One of the headlights exploded in an incandescent flare. Charlie stood there petrified, waiting for Davis to fire the round that would drop him lifeless to the ground.

The camp was enveloped in a mind-numbing silence; only the thin thread of vapor from the broken headlight gave any life whatsoever to the scene. There was a faint sound, almost a sigh, followed by a scraping rattle that comes only from deep in the lungs. Agent Davis slumped slowly into the glare of the remaining headlight and then slid silently to the ground.

Thomas was holding his left arm and making little squeaking noises, indicating to Charlie that it really hurt but was probably not fatal.

Charlie advanced on the automobile, his empty revolver still extended. He looked directly at Davis, whose glacier-blue eyes were trying to focus. He thought he perceived one final glint such as the setting sun might strike from an ice field. Charlie Yazzie was the last thing agent Davis ever saw.

~~~~~~

The next morning, Charlie and Thomas (with his arm in a sling) sat in the parking lot of the federal building and watched as prosecutors, accompanied by federal and state agencies, brought FBI agent Robert Davis's records and computer files from the building. It had taken nearly all night for the government investigators to decipher the information contained in Freddy Chee's briefcase.

Patsy Greyhorse's laptop had proven even more incriminating than LaFore's little blue disk, and it was now certain that Davis's fingerprints were on the LaFore murder weapon as well as the one used to kill Freddy Chee.

On the reservation, four high-ranking tribal officials, including Tribal Chairman Arthur Ford, were being taken into custody by federal agents out of Albuquerque. At least two of the officials had agreed to turn state's evidence, and that, along with statements taken from Charlie and Thomas, was thought to provide the proverbial "air-tight case."

The End

Follow along with Charlie and Thomas as their story continues in the next book of the series "Boy Made of Dawn" now available on Kindle or as an Amazon paperback.

We have included a bonus preview of, *Boy Made of Dawn*, as a continuation of, *Navajo Autumn*. Stay with Charlie Yazzi and Thomas Begay as stolen children and a sniper assassin bring danger and intrigue to the nation's largest reservation. Old and new characters emerge to unravel ongoing corruption. An irascible Ute family and their shrewd ranch-woman neighbor, become caught up in a plot to place certain tribal leaders above the law.

Boy Made of Dawn

R. Allen Chappell

The Rescue

Man has always felt most vulnerable in that lonely netherworld between darkness and dawn. Often it is then that death takes the sick and weak. They give up finally, unable to bear the weight of another day. A person may—not knowing why—suddenly awaken, if only for an instant, to assure himself all is well.

Charlie Yazzie woke that morning in the darkness with just such a feeling.

It was now late afternoon, and hunger was finally getting the best of him. In old Navajo when one was hungry he said, "Hunger is hurting me." Hunger was hurting Charlie now.

On his way back from Blanding—entering Bluff, Utah—he was at the very northern edge of the reservation. Legal Services had sent him to take a follow-up deposition in a domestic violence case, one originating on the Navajo reservation. It had been a wasted trip. No one at the rural address knew the plaintiff or where she might be found. Either the contact information had been wrongly transcribed, or there was a mix-up in the case files.

The only cafe in the town was nearly deserted. The girl who brought the menu and ice water seemed out of sorts, as though doing him a favor. He thought she might be *Ute*, maybe from the old *Ute* land allotments just up the road. It was just a hunch. She might as easily have been *Piute*. Charlie knew, early on, the government had scattered the few *Piute* in this area among the *Ute*, thinking them the same people. They later found this was not the case, but by that time it was too late, and they actually were pretty much the same people.

"What's good for dinner?" he asked with a smile.

She studied him for a moment, taking in the fresh shirt, pressed jeans, and shiny boots. She had watched him pull up in the new Chevrolet truck with the tribal emblem on the side. "Well, there's the Navajo taco platter," she said with a slight smirk, jabbing her finger at the number on the menu. "These people around here seem to like it." She did not smile when she said this.

He nodded, purposely taking his time now with the menu, examining it as a condemned man might contemplate his last meal. The girl, who was dark skinned and had a twitch in her left eye, tapped her foot, pencil poised. There was always this little thing between Navajo and the *Ute*. It had been going on a very long time.

It was *Ute* scouts who led Kit Carson in his roundup of the Navajo, causing their long walk to eastern New Mexico and interminable incarceration at Bosque Redondo. One hundred and fifty years later, it was still a sore subject, often vilified as the most horrifying event in Navajo history.

The Navajo taco platter actually sounded pretty good, but he would not give this rude girl the satisfaction.

"I'll have the chicken-fried steak," he said pointing at it, "with fries and extra gravy...and make that white gravy!" He wanted her to know he wasn't from around there.

Still, the smirk played at the corner of her mouth. "Salad dressing?"

"Honey mustard...if you've got it." He refused to be played.

"We got it," she declared with a curt bob of her head. "We don't get much call for it…but we got it."

"I'll have that dressing on the side, please," he added firmly.

She grimaced, writing the notation so hard she broke the pencil lead. She glared at the pencil then shot Charlie a hard look. "It'll be right out." She moved to the order window where he was pleased to see two older white women, with their hair in nets, in charge of the kitchen. He watched carefully to see she didn't do anything to his food, but she knew better.

Halfway through his dinner (which was surprisingly good) an older, rough-looking man came in and seated himself at the counter across the aisle from Charlie's table. He was a big man for an Indian. The *Ute* girl moved quickly down the counter, speaking to him in a fashion indicating a certain familiarity. They whispered for a few minutes, the man turning on his stool a time or two, looking over at Charlie. Finally, he rose and came over to the table. "My name is Hiram Buck." He didn't offer his hand. "My niece over there says that's your truck outside. Are you the law?"

Charlie put down his fork and looked the man over, finally nodding. "In a way I suppose you could say I am. I'm with Navajo Nation Legal Services." Charlie took a card from his shirt pocket and passed it to him. "Is there something I can help you with?"

"It's not me that needs help." The man looked briefly at the card. "But there's a little boy out in the canyons who I think might. I was out there today gathering some stray stock and ran across him up in an old *Anasazi* ruin back in the canyons. He can't be more than five or six years old. He ran and hid in the rocks when he saw I spotted him. My cows was getting away, and by time I had them settled he had just disappeared! He's still up there somewhere, I expect, but dammed if I could find him. Anyway, I guess someone should go up there before something happens to him." He raised his right hand as though swearing to the veracity of his statement. "There was no sign of anyone else around. I yelled and hollered but didn't get no answer." The man was becoming agitated. "It is five or six miles from the nearest road. I just can't figure out why he might be up there all alone, that's all. No one lives up that way that I know of." He paused for a moment and looked Charlie directly in the eye. "There are a couple hours of daylight left. If you want me to, I can take you back up there or at least to the corrals where I left the stock. I left my horse up there too. You could use him to ride in if you wanted to. I'll come back for the horse in the morning. I just think some kind of law should go up there and see what's what!" The man stopped to catch his breath, watching intently to see what effect all this talk might be having on Charlie.

Charlie, for his part, didn't quite know what to make of it. He suspected there was a logical explanation for the boy being out there and thought it most likely someone was looking after him. There was little doubt, however, that this man was genuinely concerned.

The man spoke again, slowly this time as though he thought Charlie might not understand what he was saying. "My Niece over there," indicating the waitress with a nod of his head, "she says the local law had to take his wife to the hospital in Cortez a couple of hours ago, and there's probably no one here in town can do anything. I think something ought to be done right now while there's still enough daylight to get back up there!"

Charlie pondered this for only a moment before putting some bills on the table. "Let's go," he said softly.

As though on signal, the man's niece took two bottles of water from the cooler and slid an apple pie into a cardboard box. She passed them to her uncle, who handed them to Charlie. "It might be a long night," was all he said.

~~~~~~

Hiram Buck knew the rutted roads like they were part of his DNA, which they probably were. Some think the *Ute* have been in that country longer than anyone—even the *Anasazi*. They were a desperately poor people in the beginning, living in small isolated family bands. They had posed little threat to those who came after, at least until much later when they got a few horses away from the Spaniards. They were the first Indians to have horses. It was not long before they were a force to be reckoned with.

Not many knew it, but Charlie had always held an interest in the pre-history of the Four Corners and its people. The University of New Mexico was a Mecca for some of the foremost scholars in the field, and he had taken classes from some of the best. More than one had tried to convince him to switch his major from law. He, however, thought he could do more good in the future than the past. He was learning of late that the two were often intertwined.

Charlie was aware many of the indigenous peoples of an area often go back to a shared gene pool. In early days there was much raiding and taking of women and children. It is sometimes difficult for latter-day ethnologists to keep the various groups separated by genetic makeup alone.

The Navajo adopted some of their culture from the ancient Pueblo peoples. Weaving and pottery making, along with rudimentary farming, were all thought to have been acquired from the Pueblos. After the introduction of sheep by the Spaniards, the Navajo took the craft of weaving to a new level. Their pottery, on the other hand, never seemed to advance beyond a plain cooking ware.

A major point of differentiation among the groups was their language rootstock affiliation: *Athabaskan* for the Navajo/Apache, *Shoshonean* for the *Ute*, and several unrelated languages for the various Pueblo peoples. No one was really certain where some of those early Pueblo people came from, though there were plenty of theories.

Some archeologists believe the *Ute* may have descended directly from the early Paleo-Indian whose bones and spear points litter the Southwest—some as old as ten thousand years or more. The *Ute* had been rubbing elbows with the Navajo and their Apache cousins for nearly a thousand years. By the latter portion of that time, the three peoples shared a number of cultural traits. Charlie knew the Navajo's genetic diversity might well be one reason they were one of the few modern tribes increasing in number.

~~~~~~

It was all Charlie could do to keep up with Hiram Buck, even with the new truck. He tried the two-way radio several times in hopes of raising someone back at dispatch. He wanted to relay his change of plans, but, as often was the case in that country, the iron-bearing cliffs deflected the signal, leaving only static and distant garbled bits and snatches of voices.

There was only about an hour of light left when they reached the trailhead. Hiram's dilapidated stock trailer was backed up to the loading chute. Three cows lounged in the weathered cedar corrals. He had tied his horse on the shady side of the trailer where there was a scattered flake of hay on the ground. Hiram had removed the saddle from the horse before leaving, which told Charlie he had not been sure when he would return. Hiram backed his truck up to the trailer and lowered the hitch onto the ball then dragged his saddle from the back of the old pickup. Charlie, meanwhile, pulled on a Levi's jacket and grabbed a blanket from the back seat of his Chevy. He also retrieved his revolver from the glove box and a folding knife he thought might come in handy. Hiram watched him out of the corner of his eye as he brought the horse around and bridled it. He left the halter and lead rope under the bridle, as is usual in that country. The saddle had a set of cheap canvas bags behind the cantle, the sort of tack auctioned off at a sale-barn before they settle on the more serious business of running the stock through.

Hiram straightened the blanket for Charlie as he hefted the saddle on and cinched it up tight, causing the gelding to groan. This horse was full of hay, and he knew the cinch would loosen quickly enough. He didn't want to stop and tighten it again if the trail got rough, and the trails in this country always got rough. Both men smiled when Charlie put the pie box in the saddlebag—that pie was in for a ride. He put the water bottles in the opposite saddlebag, tied his blanket roll over them, and was pretty much ready to go. Hiram pointed up the left fork of the trail and moved his chin in the direction of the corralled cows. "Those girls have to be at the sale barn in Cortez early in the morning...I can't afford not to have them there."

Charlie nodded and swung up on the horse with a wave of his arm to Hiram, who was already moving to load the cows.

All Charlie had to do was follow this horse's tracks back up the canyon. He thought he could make it before darkness covered the trail, provided it was no farther than Hiram Buck had said. Tall, black thunderheads gathered like a war party in the Northwest, and he eyed them with a grim resignation.

He had to kick-start the horse, who had it in mind to stay with the cows and Hiram. The gelding was none too happy to be headed back up the trail this late in the day, and with a stranger to boot. It was a good, stout horse. The *Ute* have always kept good horses.

The trail was steep and rocky for the first mile or so, and Charlie had to stop and let the horse blow at the first switchback. Once out of sight of the trailhead, the gelding put his head down, getting his mind right. Charlie wondered if Hiram might want to sell this gelding. He had been thinking of getting a horse for some time. Some believe the *Ute* are a bit rough in their horse training, but you can count on their horses to do what they are asked to do, and you don't have to ask them twice. Charlie noticed several sets of fresh horse tracks on the trail, but only old signs of cattle. Hiram must have driven his cows down the creek bed. The trail wound on up the canyon, often clinging to the side of the cliff in a rather alarming manner.

He was nearly running out of daylight when he finally urged the sorrel gelding up the cedar slope that hid the ruins. It was a small site, probably no more than ten or twelve rooms, including a couple of small granaries against the back wall. Charlie had helped do volunteer fieldwork on several sites just like it at the university. He could see by the dark line of moss at the rear of the declivity that there was a seep—enough water for a thirsty boy.

Charlie knew instinctively it would do no good to try to call the boy out in the dark. If the child had run from Hiram in the light of day, he would certainly do the same with him in the darkness. He also did not relish the thought of a precarious ride back down the canyon in the black of night. He quietly tied the gelding in the scrub oak near the ruin, rolling out his blanket in the soft duff under a juniper at the edge of the rocky walls. The boy would be watching now. Charlie hoped he would take some comfort from another human nearby. The clouds rolled in about midnight, and there was quite a display of lightning and thunder, but only a few drops of rain. There would be fear in the boy now, leaving him worn out by morning. Maybe then he would be ready to come out of hiding.

Charlie Yazzie rolled over in his blanket, turning on one side to peer at the ruins through the shadowy darkness of pre-dawn. Death was never far away for these ancient people, and now after a thousand years it again seemed to hover in the shadows.

The boy was there. Charlie could sense it. He knew time was not on his side. Another Navajo might not have lingered through a long, cold night at the edge of the ruined dwellings. Charlie Yazzie's years at government boarding school and then university had stripped away superstitious fear of the dead—or nearly so.

There was only a fine line of gray on the eastern mesas when Charlie shook off his blanket in the chill night air. He silently worked his way closer to the hollow walls, settling himself on the crumbling edge of the *kiva* to await the dawn.

As first light touched the ruins, a small, quavering voice wafted up from the depths of the overhang. The almost indiscernible words were in Navajo—it was the *Diné* blessing song sung to greet the day. Charlie's grandmother had taught him this same song as a child. This boy had been brought up by someone who still believed in the Beauty Way. It was obvious now he was Navajo. Charlie stood and raised his voice above the breeze, singing along with the boy who faltered momentarily then picked up the thread of the last verse:

Beauty above me
Beauty below me
Beauty all around me
I walk in beauty

The song is sometimes sung with slightly different words in the beginning, but always, the last verse is the same, and the little voice became stronger at the end. The boy cautiously emerged from the blackness at the back of the ruins and stood in the jumble of rocks and broken walls. Charlie averted his eyes as one would when dealing with a wild animal. Not looking directly at the boy, he retrieved the pie box and water bottles from the saddlebags. As he turned, he saw the child had come closer, standing in the warm halo of a breaking dawn. There was a glow about him as though he were made of dawn. He was a small boy for his age, which appeared to be about what Hiram Buck had reported. He was dirty (with the dust of the ruins in his hair) thin and hollow eyed. *Diné* boys are born tough, capable of enduring physical hardship at a very young age—in olden times this endurance had been a prerequisite for survival.

"Da dichin' ninizen?" Charlie asked, holding out the pie box with its jumbled contents. The boy gave a slight nod of his head and inched forward to take a handful of the wrecked apple pie. Still, he said nothing, and Charlie did not push him to talk. They ate silently, not looking at one another, and drank the water. Charlie re-saddled the horse as he watched the boy finish the crumbs. "Are your people nearby?" he asked in Navajo. The boy shook his head indicating they were not. Charlie mounted the horse and offered the boy a hand up; he did not hesitate but swung up behind in silence.

As they rode down the shadowed canyon trail in the cool of early morning, Charlie was glad the boy was at least wearing a heavy sweatshirt. The offer of his jacket had been refused. The *Ute* horse cautiously picked his way down a particularly rough stretch. As is often the case, the trail was more treacherous going down than coming up. Again, it occurred to Charlie what a fine horse this was. Not so much for looks, but it had good sense and was broke for anyone who could sit up straight and ride. They eased their way down toward a trickle of water meandering through a thin band of young cottonwoods. The horse had not drunk that morning, and Charlie let him leave the main trail and follow a well-beaten path to the stream. He could see by the tracks that this horse had watered there the previous day.

The boy slid off, and Charlie dismounted and loosened the girth, lowering the reins so the horse might drink his fill; it might be his last drink that day. The boy moved downstream to a little patch of oak brush to relieve himself. Charlie smiled at this bit of backcountry etiquette from one so young. He pulled the empty water bottles from the saddlebags, intending to fill them from the clear pool beside the horse. As he went down on one knee and leaned over to fill the bottles, the horse suddenly tossed his head and whinnied, jerking back on the reins, causing Charlie to lose his balance and sprawl backwards in the tall grass. It was at that instant a rifle shot exploded—a geyser of water erupting just where Charlie had knelt the moment before. Instinctively, he rolled sideways into the cover of the willows and called for the boy to get down. As the shot echoed down the canyon, he momentarily lost track of the boy. The horse had jerked loose and now, confused, stepped forward into the water; he did not bolt but stood transfixed, staring across the narrow canyon. He was blocking Charlie's view but offered enough cover to crawl toward the boy. They met behind a large boulder that lay half in the stream. Charlie pulled the boy to him, shielding him with his own body. His pistol was out of the shoulder holster, and he held it out away from the boy, who was shivering now. Charlie himself was trembling and placed the boy beside him, back against the rock, his arm still around him. That shot had come from a good distance, and he knew his .38 would not have the range to confront this person, who was obviously a very good shot. That horse had saved his life, to his way of thinking. After a few minutes of numbing silence, Charlie could hear the faint, far-off metallic clatter of a shod horse's hooves on slick rock.

Maybe the shooter thought Charlie had been hit when he was thrown backwards; or maybe he just figured he had missed his chance and had best get away while he could; or maybe the shooter's horse had run off without him, and he was up there waiting for another shot. He looked over at the boy, who gave a little half-grin and shrugged his shoulders. This made Charlie smile. This boy would do well someday, given half a chance.

Charlie waited as long as he could stand it and then indicated to the boy that he should stay put. He rolled sideways into the oak brush for a view of the rim without being seen. He studied the area he thought the shot had come from and noted, directly across from them, an old, fallen spruce log well out on the otherwise bare sandstone point. It was only about two hundred yards as the crow flies—the canyon narrowed that much at this point. Perfect place for an ambush for someone who knew how to shoot, he thought. After a few more minutes, he cautiously stood up, ready to hit the dirt at the first sign of movement. Keeping an eye on the rim, he eased over and picked up the reins to the horse. It had lowered its head and was now calmly cropping grass. Charlie thought this was the kind of horse a man might be able to shoot off of—should the need arise. His grandfather had often cautioned him there was never any justification for shooting off a horse; there were very few that would stand for it. He tightened the cinch and, after another careful look around, called to the boy, who rose up and came over, ready to clamber back aboard.

Back on the trail, Charlie's mind raced as he searched every tree and boulder ahead. He couldn't help but notice a number of horse tracks coming and going on this trail, both shod and unshod. He studied the tracks with the skill earned following run-off stock as a boy. The sign was clear to him once he had let his mind return to that time when being a tracker was something of value. Again, it struck him as odd that there were no fresh cow tracks, and he pondered the possibilities. A shadow of trepidation made for a much slower return, though the horse was now champing at the bit, anxious to be fed, and possibly looking forward to a little equine company. No matter the training, a horse is a herd animal, a trait any real horseman keeps always in the front of his mind. As they neared the trailhead, Charlie scanned the path ahead, halting occasionally to survey the terrain.

He could sense the boy grow nervous again, felt him flinch and hold tight as the horse nickered and shook himself at the sight of the corrals. Something bad had happened here, and it was running through the boys mind. He still had not spoken a word. There would be plenty of time for that later; now, he needed to get this boy back to town.

He also needed to call Sue Hanagarni, who he had promised to meet for breakfast this morning. Shiprock and the Dinè Bikeyah Cafe were still some hours down the road.

He saw Hiram had left a couple of flakes of hay for the horse. The *Ute* would probably be back for it after he finished at the sale-barn in Cortez. Hiram Buck had gone to a lot of trouble for this boy. Charlie intended to let him know later how it all turned out.

The boy slid off the horse and immediately went to open the corral gate for Charlie—he had obviously spent time around stock and was anxious to pitch in and help. Charlie liked this boy. He could see a lot of himself in him when he was young. They stashed the tack out of sight behind the corral and sat in the pickup truck for a few minutes while Charlie once again tried, unsuccessfully, to reach someone on the radio. He noticed the boy, out of the corner of his eye, entranced by the truck's multi-lighted instrument panel and radio controls. The boy was enumerating each of them with a tentative forefinger as though trying to understand their function. Most Indian boys love pickup trucks as their fore-fathers loved horses. They are the path to being a man, they think.

Charlie took the cutoff. When he hit the flats out of Aneth, he radioed the switchboard and had the operator forward a message to Sue Hanagarni: they had best meet for lunch instead of breakfast. They had known one another since boarding school and had worked together in Legal Services for two years now. Sue was an easygoing girl, but he knew he would have some explaining to do. He thought he would ask Sue to marry him at some point.

Charlie turned on 160 to Teec Nos Pos then dropped down on 64 toward Shiprock. As the miles slipped by, he once or twice tried to engage the boy in conversation, first in English and then Navajo, but could get no more than a nod or shake of his head in return. There was something haunt-ingly familiar about this boy he could not get out of his head. Maybe it was because he had been much the same himself as a youngster.

They had to pass right by his place on the way into town. He thought they had time to clean up a bit and maybe give the boy's clothes a quick wash on half cycle. The clothes were still a bit damp when they left, but it was warm out, and there was no help for it. Sue would be waiting at the Dinè Bikeyah Cafe—and she wouldn't wait long.

When they pulled up to the restaurant, her old Datsun pickup was in the parking lot right next to the entrance, which meant she had arrived early before the Saturday lunch crowd. The boy looked better cleaned up—his hair slicked down with a little Wildroot Cream Oil that Charlie kept for his cowlick when it acted up. The boy was not used to being all spruced up. He kept looking at his image in the truck's side mirror; he gave no sign he liked what he saw.

They spotted Sue at a far table by a window and came up on her while she studied the menu. When she looked up, she at first did not see the child standing slightly behind Charlie.

"Well, it's about ti…" Her greeting trailed off as she saw the boy peeking out from behind him. The boy shrugged his shoulders at the surprised look on her face.

"This is…well, I don't know who he is," Charlie offered, nudging the boy forward.

Sue smiled. "What! Did he follow you home?" She turned the smile on the boy. "What's your name, fella?" The boy dropped his head and did not answer. "Oh, a shy guy, huh? Well, that's all right. I like the strong, silent type…so unlike some people I know," she said casting Charlie a sideways glance, but still smiling.

"What? I'm strong!" Charlie flexed his biceps. He eased the boy into the booth ahead of him and moved one of the silverware packets over in front of him. "I'll bet you're hungry again, huh?"

Sue thought the boy awfully thin. "When did he eat last?"

"Well, he had a scrambled apple pie for breakfast about daylight, but that's about it. I don't think he's had a whole lot to eat lately."

Sue raised her eyebrows. "Whole apple pie, huh? That ought to put some meat on his bones."

Charlie laughed. "I helped him with the pie…but you'd be surprised."

"I'll bet," Sue grinned back. She had already selected lunch so passed him the menu. She was glad to see Charlie and wanted him to know it. She touched his hand across the table. "Does he talk at all?" she asked.

"No, but he can sing a blue streak…when he wants too." He turned to the boy. "What's it going to be, guy?" The boy said nothing. "How about a big cheese burger and some fries with ketchup?" The boy looked down at the table, but a hint of a smile crossed his lips.

After the waitress took their orders, Charlie launched into the story of how he had come by the boy, who stared out the window rather than see the sad look on Sue's face as she listened. Charlie left out the part about the shooting. The food came, and the boy tucked into his with a will. Charlie unwrapped the silverware for him, but the boy—engrossed in the food—paid no attention. "I was surprised he came to me." Charlie said around a mouthful of burger. "Him not knowing me and all."

The boy turned and looked at Charlie. "I know you," he said softly. "You are Thomas Begay's friend!"

Charlie spluttered and almost dropped his fork. He cocked his head at the boy. "How do you know Thomas Begay?" he said forgetting to speak Navajo. And then it hit him. "And I know who you are too now, *atsilí*!" He put his fork down and looked across the table at Sue, who was staring open-mouthed at them. "This is Sally Klee's boy from over by Farmington. You remember, Thomas Begay's "friend" from the Greyhorse case last fall!"

Sue raised her eyebrows, staring at the boy, and then nodded. "I remember."

"Well, let's finish lunch," he said with a quick glance at Sue, who nodded.

Charlie thought it best to let the thing lie; this would be something best left alone until Thomas Begay was present. The bright spot was, the boy would not now have to be turned over to Social Services—not just yet anyway.

In the parking lot Charlie had the boy stay in the truck while he and Sue stepped away to talk.

"Busy this afternoon?" he asked.

She shook her head.

"Good. Want to take a ride out to Thomas's? I think we need to have a little chat. I'm wondering now where Sally and this boy's sister are."

Sue was up for it, and the boy scooted right over when she got in the truck.

Thomas and Lucy Tallwoman had become good friends since the Greyhorse affair. The four of them now occasionally met in town for dinner at Denny's or sometimes had cookouts at Lucy's place. Sue and Charlie had both known Thomas since boarding school in Aztec and had been close; then Charlie went away to law school, and Thomas's drinking took control of his life. Thomas did not drink now. Lucy Tallwoman had become a friend of Sue's, and on the way out to her camp, Sue caught Charlie's eye. Looking over the boy's head, she silently mouthed the question, "Does Lucy know about this boy?"

Charlie mirrored her quizzical expression and shrugged his shoulders. He had never discussed the matter with Thomas beyond the time Thomas had admitted the boy and his sister were his. It had happened long before he had known Lucy Tallwoman; he did not think Thomas would have told her.

Charlie's mind ranged back to that autumn afternoon when he and Thomas had gone out to Sally Klee's *hogan* under the bluffs outside Farmington. They had been looking for her half brother Freddy Chee but wound up with more than they bargained for, including a briefcase full of evidence that proved instrumental in bringing down a number of very important people—people who would be coming to trial soon. He remembered Sally as a small, thin young woman who spoke English like his grandmother. She was probably no more than twenty-five years old at the time. He recalled her half brother Freddy Chee had earlier given her a beating to insure her silence. Still, she had risked telling Thomas what she knew of Freddie's part in the matter. She had also told him she was leaving that place and going to live with her cousins. Charlie doubted she ever moved back to that old *hogan*. Freddie had died a violent and lonely death there. His *chindi* would still be trapped in that *Hogan*—and the *chindi* of a *yeenaaldiooshii* is not to be trifled with. Neither she nor any other Navajo would ever live in that *hogan* again.

~~~~~~

Lucy Tallwoman's old father Paul T'Sosi was just bringing the sheep down from the cedar hills behind the *hogan* when they pulled up in the yard. The boy perked up immediately and watched intently through the windshield as the dog worked the sheep into the corrals. He glanced at Charlie and smiled. It seemed plain the boy had the primal instinct to follow the herds—it was part of who he was.

The old man waved but finished with the sheep before coming over. *"Ya' eh t'eeh,"* he called even before reaching the truck. Charlie heard the old man had not been well these last few weeks, but he looked fine now. He was smiling as he patted the hood of the new Chevy. "This is more like it," he grinned. "Legal Services is finally stepping up, huh."

Charlie laughed and pointed to the blue Dodge truck next to the *hogan*. "I see you finally got another truck too!" He knew it was really Lucy's truck, but the polite thing was to acknowledge the old man's part in the thing.

"Oh, Thomas Begay got tired of hay-wiring that old one back together, I guess. He picked it out. He just had to have a diesel. I don't know where he plans to plug it in this winter; we can't run the generator all night just so this truck will start." He had slipped in the part about their having a new generator as an indicator of how well they were doing. Paul had come up to the window now, and Charlie could see he truly wasn't pleased with Thomas's choice of a truck.

"The salesman told us it would pull a *hogan* off its foundation…going uphill…into the wind!" He spit in the dust. "I don't know why anyone would want to pull their *hogan* off its foundation," and then as an afterthought, "anyways, *hogans* don't even have foundations." They both laughed at this, and the old man shook his head. "That Thomas," he grinned. "At least he's not drinking anymore, and he's making a little money right along, too."

Charlie nodded. "That's good!" There really wasn't much more he could say about that.

Sue peeked around Charlie and waved at the old man. "Hi there! The sheep are looking good! Is Lucy still working on the *Ye'i* blanket?"

Paul liked Sue and couldn't understand why she and Charlie hadn't gotten married yet; they were together all the time, and he liked to tease them about it whenever he got the chance. "She's still working on it. I expect that's what she's doing right now. At least she was when I left with the sheep this morning." Paul turned his attention to the boy between them. "Who's that little guy?"

"That's what we're about to find out, I hope. Is Thomas around?"

"Should be up by now. He had to work most of last night for the road crew on a washout up the road."

The boy perked up at the mention of Thomas's name. "Thomas," he whispered to himself, but no one heard.

Charlie and Sue got out of the truck, leaving the boy in the front seat watching them, and with the old man trailing behind, slowly made their way up to the *hogan*. They figured Lucy Tallwoman already knew they were there but wanted to give her a few minutes. Spur-of-the-moment visits were the norm in this country, but Sue knew Lucy would appreciate at least a few minutes.

Thomas Begay appeared at the open door, bleary-eyed and tired looking, to welcome them. He held a cup of coffee in one hand and flipped his long hair out of his eyes with the other. Charlie moved forward. "Sorry to spring this on you, *hastiin*, but we didn't know what else to do." Charlie indicated the Chevy with a twist of his head.

"Spring what?" Thomas looked from one to the other of them. "What are you talking about?"

The boy, arms folded on the dashboard, stared silently out the windshield at Thomas. When Thomas glanced over at the truck, he calmly placed his coffee cup down on the water barrel by the door and moved past them to the Chevy. The others fell silent and looked away as he opened the door and lifted the little boy out, standing him on the ground he straightened his shirt. Together, the two of them walked toward the corrals, Thomas speaking softly in Navajo and the boy nodding his head from time to time.

Lucy came to the door smiling at her unexpected guests. "This is a nice surprise..." She stopped in midsentence as she saw Thomas and the boy watching the sheep together. Her face clouded for an instant, but she immediately regained her composer, motioning everyone into the *hogan*.

Sue instantly took up the slack by exclaiming loudly over the weaving loom set up inside the door, "Oh, Lucy! It's nearly done. How do you do it? I thought it would take forever!" As Lucy and Sue examined the blanket in its final stages of weaving, Lucy showed her the tiny imperfection purposely woven into the warp of one corner. It was thought the weaver became part of the piece during the creation. Sue knew this almost imperceptible thread at the lower corner of the blanket was done to allow the weavers spirit to escape, insuring she could detach her spirit from the piece and let it go. It is a tradition common in most Navajo art.

(End of preview)

The complete *Boy Made of Dawn*, is available now on Kindle or in paperback at:

http://www.amazon.com/dp/B00F4DIJ10/

ABOUT THE AUTHOR

Writer, poet R. Allen Chappell's work has appeared in many magazines, literary and poetry publications, and has been featured on public radio and television.

Navajo Autumn is the first book in his Navajo Nation mystery series. *Boy Made of Dawn* is the second novel in the trilogy. Look for his latest book in the spring of 2014.

An unrelated short story collection *The Fat of the Land* is on Amazon in both paperback and Kindle.

Chappell grew up in New Mexico at the edge of the great reservation where he still maintains many friendships. He and his wife spend most winters on a small sailboat in Mexico and summers at home in Colorado where he pursues an active interest in the archeology and anthropology of the Southwest. He welcomes reader comments at:

rachappell@yahoo.com

If you have enjoyed this book, please go to the Amazon book page and leave a short review. It would be most appreciated.

http://www.amazon.com/dp/B00BOZ3WH8/

Appendix

Glossary

1. Ashiihi.........................Salt People (clan) *
2. Billigaana.......................white people
3. Chindi (or chinde)...............spirit of the dead *
4. Dinè..............................Navajo people
5. Dinè Bikeyah...................Navajo country
6. Haltsooi........................Meadow Clan
7. Hataalii........................Shaman (Singer)*
8. Hastiin (Hosteen)...............man
9. Hogan...........................traditional dwelling
10. Hozo............................to walk in beauty *
11. Yaa' eh t'eeh...................greeting - hello
12. Yeenaaldiooshii................Skinwalker, witch,*
13. Ye'i............................spirit-helper

See notes*

Notes

1. *Ashiihi - The Salt People are thought to be the most numerous clan affiliation in the Navajo Mountain area. Old White Man Killer was an early and powerful Salt People clan resident of the area, coming there in 1892. He is thought to have many descendants.

3. *Chindi – (or chinde) When a person dies inside a hogan, it is said that his chindi or spirit remains there forever, causing the hogan to be abandoned. Chindi are not considered benevolent entities. For the traditional Navajo, just speaking a dead person's name may call up his chindi and cause harm to the speaker.

7. *Hataalii – Generally known as a "Singer" among the Dinè, these men are considered "Holy Men" and have apprenticed to older practitioners, sometimes for many years, to learn the ceremonies. They make the sand-paintings that are an integral part of the healing and know the many songs which must be sung in the correct order.

10. *Hozo – For the Navajo "hozo" (sometimes hozoji) is a general state of well-being (both physical and spiritual) that indicates a certain "state of grace," which is referred to as "walking in beauty." Illness or depression is the usual cause of "loss of hozo," which put's one out of sync with the people as a whole. There are ceremonies to restore hozo and return the ailing person to a oneness with his people.

12. *Yeenaaldiooshii – These witches, as they are often referred to, are the chief source of evil or fear in the traditional Navajo superstitions. They are thought to be capable of many unnatural acts, such as flying, or turning themselves into werewolves and other ethereal creatures, hence the term Skinwalkers, referring to their ability to change forms or skins.

13. *Ye'i – A generally benevolent spirit-helper, often seen depicted in weavings and sand-paintings. At major "Sings" or ceremonies, men dressed as ye'i's go among the crowd as helper-beggars and provide a valuable service to the Hataalii performing the ceremony.

Made in the USA
San Bernardino, CA
23 February 2014